I've travelled the world twice over,
Met the famous: saints and sinners,
Poets and artists, kings and queens,
Old stars and hopeful beginners,
I've been where no-one's been before,
Learned secrets from writers and cooks
All with one library ticket
To the wonderful world of books.

© JANICE JAMES.

GUILT WITHOUT PROOF

In less than twenty-four hours Fortrow CID have two problems on their hands — the hijacking of a lorry-load of whisky and the discovery of a man's body in the burnt-out cellar of a wine shop. Are the two events connected? The police think 'yes', but when their theory is exploded it takes a lot of painstaking work, a little rule-bending and a slice of luck before Detective Inspector Fusil arrives at the truth. But knowing the culprit is not enough: they then need the proof to convict him.

PETER ALDING

$\blacklozenge$

GUILT
WITHOUT
PROOF

Complete and Unabridged

ULVERSCROFT
Leicester

First published in Great Britain in 1970 by
John Long Limited
London

First Large Print Edition
published July 1991

British Library CIP Data

Alding, Peter. *1926 –*
Guilt without proof. — Large print ed. —
Ulverscroft large print series: mystery
I. Title
823.914[F]

ISBN 0–7089–2456–5

Published by
F. A. Thorpe (Publishing) Ltd.
Anstey, Leicestershire

Set by Words & Graphics Ltd.
Anstey, Leicestershire
Printed and bound in Great Britain by
T. J. Press (Padstow) Ltd., Padstow, Cornwall

1

THE van, swaying quickly, overtook a saloon car halfway up the hill.

"Steady it up, Ginger," ordered Stretley. "Keep going like this and the pigs'll have us for speeding."

"Stop sweating," muttered Playford, the driver.

Stretley, sitting athwartships on the floor of the compartment, spoke more harshly: "Slow down, I said."

Playford eased off the accelerator. "We ought've come up to the lorry."

Finnigan, in the passenger seat, laughed. "Maybe the driver's got a hot judy waitin' and 'as been burning up the roads."

There was a sharp blast of a car's horn and a Jensen went past at well over the legal maximum.

Finnigan whistled. "D'you see the judy in that car? There's some ripe 'omework, and no mistake." He had two topics of conversation: women and the dogs.

They reached the brow of the hill and

began the gentle descent. The road made a sharp right turn half a mile on and then ran straight up to the brow of a small rise. A lorry had just rounded the bend.

"Is that our truck?" said Playford, his voice a shade louder.

Neither of the other two answered. At this distance, it was impossible to identify the lorry.

Finnigan began to whistle. He stopped in the middle of a bar. "Look, I say we wait on where we leave the truck and find out who collects it."

"No," snapped Stretley.

"That way, we makes ourselves some extra . . . "

"We're not staying," shouted Stretley.

Finnigan swore, but then suddenly grinned. He was good-looking in a wild, reckless way: it was easy to judge that he knew little self-control.

It took them eight minutes to come up to the lorry and when they were within a hundred yards of it they could see the name on the canvas: 'E. Phillpot & Co.' It was not the one they were after. Playford accelerated and they overtook it.

Stretley unwrapped a stick of chewing-gum and put it in his mouth. He chewed rapidly. He was the oldest of the three and his square face was marked with vicious lines: he had served three terms of imprisonment for G.B.H. As they passed under a railway bridge, he said: "Fifteen miles to go." His voice was worried. They should have come up to the lorry by Barstone by-pass.

There were road-works just beyond Peston crossroads and the single-line traffic was controlled by portable traffic lights which were changing too rapidly to allow many vehicles through at any one time. The driver of a Mini ignored the red light and tried to force his way against the oncoming traffic. Immediately, there was a snarl-up that took several minutes to sort itself out. As they waited, Playford swore as he fidgeted with the wheel and Stretley kept looking at his watch: only Finnigan seemed careless of the delay.

"I told you we should've moved earlier," said Playford harshly.

"We'll get moving now," snapped Stretley, as the car in front of them began to pull away.

Playford let out the clutch too abruptly and the engine stalled.

Finnigan laughed. "I'll get out and put up the L-plates."

Playford for once said nothing. He was bigger and stronger than Finnigan, but would never willingly mix it with the other: Finnigan's air of recklessness suggested that when really angered he could become almost berserk.

They drove forward. Stretley looked at his watch again. They should have met up with the lorry long before now, which would have let them get to the café vehicle-park first, but it now seemed almost certain they wouldn't. Perhaps the lorry had even left the café and was in Fortrow. If so, they'd lost out on a thousand quid.

The van began to sway again as Playford increased speed, but this time Stretley gave no order to slow down.

"Maybe the dope was sour," said Playford suddenly.

"It's been good before."

"There's always a first time," said Finnigan lightly.

A white police patrol car passed in the opposite direction. Playford swore at it, with childish hatred and defiance. Then he floored the accelerator as he saw two lorries ahead. Bucking and swaying, the van came up to the lorries: neither was their quarry.

Stretley lowered the window and spat out the chewing-gum. Goddamn it, he thought, was this job really going to turn sour? He needed his share of that thousand and needed it bad: he owed a lot on the horses and if he didn't pay soon, Lou was going to send someone to collect and the half-chivs would be out.

"There's the caff," said Playford suddenly. He braked.

The Jack of Hearts was one of the most popular of the many cafés on the London-Fortrow road and from early morning to late night its park was filled with lorries and the occasional car.

"Drive in," ordered Stretley.

Playford put up the indicator arm and braked again. He pulled into the park and drove past an articulated lorry piled high with crates that were marked for Sydney, a bulk milk tanker, and a pantechnicon van. The free space curved round and Playford had begun to turn when Finnigan suddenly said: "There it is."

The lorry, medium-sized and obviously nearly new, was parked end on to the tumbledown post-and-rail fencing. On the tarpaulin which covered the load was printed the name, 'MacLaren Distilleries, Machrihanish.'

"Keep going," said Stretley, as Playford braked almost to a stop.

"But we . . . "

"I said, keep going." Stretley was determined to make quite certain there were no general security defences and that no tip-off had brought the police here to hide and wait.

They completed the rough semi-circle to the road and the second entrance and Stretley had seen nothing remotely suspicious. "O. K.," he said.

Playford drove out of the entrance and along the road, past the crudely painted sign of a Jack of Hearts to the first entrance and he once more went into the park. They stopped in front of the lorry from Machrihanish.

Each of them checked on the gloves he was wearing, making certain they were untorn even though each had satisfied himself on this point before beginning the journey and in any case the gloves were new. Finnigan and Stretley were wearing hats whose brims masked much of the upper parts of their heads and overalls that were dirty with grease and dirt and bore the legend 'Dunlop'.

Playford remained at the wheel of the van. He tried to act as if this job was as easy as lifting a packet of fags from a chain-store, but could not stop fiddling with the gear lever. Finnigan slid back his door and stepped out: Stretley, carrying a metal tool-box, scrambled over the seat and followed him. On each side of the van was a printed notice which said 'Bowen and Co. Heavy transport repairs. Ring Fortrow 291698.'

They approached the lorry's cab from opposite sides. The driver might be inside. They were ready to use whatever force was necessary, but found the cab was empty.

Stretley lay down on the ground on his back and wriggled his way under the engine and cab. He switched on a small torch and used the beam to search for wires which would pin-point an alarm attached to the cab door, but there was none. He moved back and scrambled to his feet and nodded.

Finnigan came round the front of the lorry to stand between him and the L-shaped café. Because of the closeness with which the vehicles were parked, they had a great deal of cover.

Stretley took a bunch of keys from his pocket and tried them in turn. The last one fitted and released the door lock. He slid open the cab door and climbed up into the cab.

There was an umbrella-type lock fixed to the steering wheel. "Cutters," he said.

Finnigan picked out a pair of very strong bolt cutters from the tool kit and handed them up. Stretley tried to cut through the metal upright, but could make little impression on the specially hardened steel, even when his muscles began to shake from the intensity of his effort. "Extension."

Finnigan passed up two extension arms that fitted on to the cutter. Stretley turned the cutter round until they could each apply force to one arm. Both knew how dangerous this moment was to them — no one seeing them could be fooled into believing they were just carrying out repairs. Gradually, the cutters bit through the upright, finishing with a sudden snap that caught them completely off balance and threw them into each other so that their heads clashed.

Finnigan removed the extension arms and replaced them and the cutter in the tool kit. He then leaned into the cab and tried to give the impression of a mechanic hard at work. Stretley used his torch to check under the dashboard and found some wiring that had clearly been installed after the lorry was built. He cut the wiring, satisfied it fed an alarm. Finnigan stepped back.

Stretley started the engine. The heavy diesel thumped into life. He backed and turned, a shade too sharply because the side of the lorry scraped along the cab of the articulated vehicle alongside. There was a muted screech of metal. He cursed, stopped the lorry, went forward and altered the lock, and then backed again. This time, all was clear.

As he braked for the road, he looked in the large rear-view mirror. All seemed quiet and undisturbed. The van followed him smoothly, showing Playford was unworried. Stretley drew out into the road and turned left.

A quarter of a mile along were crossroads and to the left was sign-posted the chest hospital, a jumble of buildings halfway up the hill and just visible from the road. Stretley turned into the side road and this soon became no more than a lane, so that the sides of the lorry were constantly battering against the overhanging trees. Twice, oncoming cars had to draw into shallow passing-points to enable the lorry to get by.

At the top of the hill was a T-junction. He turned right and in half a mile came to a belt of trees. There was a natural lay-by and from this a rough track led into the woods. The track curled round out of sight of the road, then stopped abruptly against a wall of rioting brambles, bracken, weed grass, rose-bay willowherb, and sapling growth. He switched off the engine and jumped down from the cab. As he began to walk back up the track, he saw Finnigan coming towards him. His expression became ugly.

"Couldn't've been neater," said Finnigan.

"Where are you going?" demanded Stretley roughly.

"I told you — I'm staying around to find out the name of the bloke what's making all the big folding money."

"Don't be such a bloody fool."

"Listen, Abe, a thousand quid ain't much between three. We could make . . . "

"Get on back to the van."

"No," said Finnigan and he smiled crookedly.

Stretley swore, but recognised that unless he were to use force there was nothing he could do. He hesitated, then pushed roughly past the other.

2

THE candle slowly burned down. Wax overflowed and instead of being consumed by the flame it spilled out over the yellow-black powdery mixture so that for the moment the flame, which was reflected on all sides in quick stabs of light, could not reach the home-made gunpowder.

On the stone floor lay a man. He was breathing heavily, almost snoring, and from time to time he jerked his hands and legs in involuntary movements. Once, he made a noise that was half moan, half sigh.

The candle burned on, the flame wavering only slightly in the almost calm air. Some of the melted wax was burned away to leave the powder exposed. The flame seemed drawn towards the powder. There was a violent ball of fire which engulfed the candle and flashed out across the floor and up to the ceiling.

The ceiling was wooden. No sooner had

the fire touched it than the wooden joists and planks began to burn with an ever-increasing intensity. The temperature rose quickly. The man began to jerk violently, as if deep within his drugged mind there was responsive reasoning left which was trying to force him into some action to save his life. Sweat prickled his face and, until it was dried by the ever increasing heat, his wet skin glistened.

His clothes smouldered, then caught fire. His hair shrivelled up. His limbs jerked wildly and a tormented groan came from between his drawn-back lips.

Kerr looked at his reflection in the mirror and grinned at himself. For all of twelve hours now, he'd been engaged. The feeling was far better than a night on the wallop — and, come to that, there was no hang-over to mar the pleasure. He turned away from the mirror and became thoughtful. Engagements raised problems. He needed an engagement ring. Franks, in the High Street, had some magnificent diamond engagement rings there was usually one on display in a window, guarded by a fine steel grille . . .

He walked in and spoke to the tailor's dummy of an assistant in a lordly voice. The largest and best and to hell with the expense. The diamond he chose was the size of a pigeon's egg. It dazzled with its brilliance. When he gave the ring to Helen, she could do nothing but stare at it with wild-eyed astonishment . . . He sighed. Engagement rings, even the most modest ones, called for money. He had a pound or two in the Post Office savings, four quid in his wallet, and a P.C. at the station who owed him ten bob. That lot put together wouldn't buy a brass ring set with the tiniest zircon.

His depression was transitory. Engagement rings apart, life was wonderful. He couldn't think why he hadn't become engaged before. A bachelor was a man only half living.

He tied his tie, put on his coat and, whistling cheerfully, went down to the canteen. The hostel canteen was staffed by the same type of lady as the police station canteen — What d'you want, it's all gone, there ain't anything else, and I'm not working myself to the bone for no one. He asked for kippers, eggs, bacon, and liver, and was served with two tired eggs and one piece of frizzled bacon. He carried the tray over to a table at which sat a uniformed P.C.

"'Morning, Cock," he said, "lovely day!"

The P.C. turned and looked out of the window. "Are you tight again? Can't you see it's raining?"

"Is it?" Kerr shrugged his shoulders.

"You're a bright ray of sunshine. Doesn't matter to you that I've got to patrol in the wet, does it?"

"My heart bleeds for you."

"Just what the hell is up with you, John?"

"I'm celebrating my coming release from meals in this flaming canteen."

The P.C. showed interest. "Don't say you're clearing out of the force, then? What are you going for? A job at one of the factories, thirty quid a week, and a nice strike every other month?"

"Not me, chum. I'm getting married."

The P.C. laughed.

"What's so funny about that?"

"You getting married? You're the one who always said that any bloke with an ounce of sense had his cake and ate it and then moved on to find another slice."

"If ever you mature, you'll learn there's more to life than sex."

The P.C. pushed his plate to one side and stood up. "You can count me out if it means ending up like you." He left.

Kerr buttered a piece of toast, slid it under the eggs, and ate. The eggs tasted as anaemic as they looked. When he was married to Helen, his fried eggs would be cooked to perfection and when he left the house to go to work he would receive a loving kiss instead of a glare of dislike from the old harridan behind the counter.

He left the hostel at twenty past eight, totally unworried that he must arrive late at the station. To a newly engaged man, time was of small consequence. Detective Inspector Fusil disagreed on this point.

"You're late," Fusil said, as Kerr reported to his office.

"I had to wait a long time for the bus, sir."

"That's your concern, not mine." Fusil was lean and sharp looking and his appearance correctly mirrored his character. If keenness could be a fault, he suffered from it. He pulled a piece of paper across

16

his desk and glanced down at it. "There was a fire in Verlay's Wine Store in Chertain Road early this morning and the report's come in that a body's been found in the rubble. Get out there and see if this concerns us." Fusil looked up. "And keep your mind on the job — not wherever it is you so often leave it."

Kerr left and went along to the C.I.D. general room to collect his mackintosh. He didn't speak to Rowan, who sat at his desk typing, because the other was very plainly in one of his ill humours. Rowan, he thought, usually was.

For once, the ancient C.I.D. Hillman was parked in the courtyard and Kerr opened the driving door and climbed inside. He switched on and pressed the starter and was surprised when the engine fired immediately. It might be raining, he thought, but this was one of those days when everything would go right. He drove out of the courtyard, but had to wait for the traffic to ease off before pulling out into the road. How cheaply could one buy a respectable engagement ring? And how could he have wasted so much precious money in the past on beer and skittles?

The wine store in Chertain Road, a three-storey building sandwiched between an ironmongers and a greengrocers, looked strangely pathetic with windows gaping and brickwork blackened: good living had suddenly been scorched out of existence. He parked by the metal 'Police No Parking' sign, then pushed his way through a crowd of onlookers. The P.C. guarding the doorway jerked his thumb inside. "The stiff's down below in the cellar," he said crudely. "Watch how you go or you'll make the second one."

The floor had burned away from a point just beyond the counter and a ladder had been placed to give access below. Kerr climbed down the ladder. The cellar was filled with a mass of sodden, charred rubble and pieces of glass from the hundreds of shattered bottles. Most of the water had been pumped out, but some still lay around in puddles. The smell was both acrid and sickly sweet, a mixture of fire and highly aromatic liqueurs. Work had begun in clearing some of the rubble, then the body had been discovered.

Kerr stared at the body and tried to view it unemotionally, but he had not learned how to separate the sight of death from the knowledge of the pain and suffering which had preceded it. One arm was raised over the face and one of the legs was slightly crooked, in the classic pugilistic attitude that looked so much like a last vain attempt at physical defence rather than what it was, the result of the final muscular contraction. The face was completely blackened and practically without features: the mouth was open and the teeth looked white so that it macabrely seemed as if he were smiling.

A fireman, with the two shoulder pips of a station officer, clambered over the debris and came up to Kerr. "Nothing's been touched from the moment we found the body."

Grimly, Kerr thought that there could have been no greater contrast between his mood of elated happiness earlier that morning and his present sense of revulsion at the sight of the person, almost certainly male, who had burned to death. Why, he wondered with angry resentment, did there have to be tragedy in life and death?

There was a job to be done and he forced himself to do it. He searched round as much of the body as was exposed, careful not to disturb it. Most of the clothing had been burned away, or charred to the point of disintegration, but it was fairly certain from one scrap that had escaped that the shirt had been a light green. He could see no signs of violence.

When he had finished, Kerr spoke to the station officer. "Have you any idea who lived upstairs and whether he's missing?"

"The manager and his wife live there. The wife discovered the fire and her husband telephoned the alarm. When the pump arrived, they were out on the pavement scared three parts silly." The station officer spoke wearily. "We stopped the fire from burning out the upper floors, but I'd say the shell of the building has been too badly damaged for anyone to go back to living there."

"D'you know where the two of them have gone?"

"They told one of my blokes they were going to their married daughter until things get sorted out. They gave him the address. It's that chap over there." He pointed to a leading fireman who was standing in the far corner of the cellar.

Kerr clambered over the wreckage and

spoke to the leading fireman, who gave him the address. He wrote it down. "How did they take the news of the dead body in the cellar?"

"They was too bewildered to say or do anything," replied the other. "They all gets like that when their place goes up in smoke." He sounded as if he could not understand this. "I suppose you've had a look at the grating up there?" He jerked his head in the direction of the wall to their right.

"No — what about it?"

"You haven't seen it — and you're the detective?"

Kerr ignored the other's facetiousness and went round to examine the grating. The roof of the cellar was set three feet above the level of the ground outside. Most of this three feet was a brick wall, but in the centre had been a half-moon window which opened from the bottom upwards and inwards. Outside were iron bars to guard the window and the two centre ones had been forced apart to the point where they touched the bars next to them. Clearly there had been a break in, and in all probability the body was

21

that of the intruder. Kerr turned back and looked at the body and this time he knew little revulsion at the sight: although quite illogical, the knowledge that the dead man had probably been a thief lessened by far the disgust at the nature of the death.

"If you ask me, Mr. Holmes," said the fireman, with leaden humour, "someone came in here for a quick tot and ended up with more than he bargained for."

"What started the fire?"

"These old places are like tinder-boxes. Show 'em half a naked light and they break out in flames."

"But this must have been a hell of a fire?"

"This one? Doesn't make the grade. Now I was out at a fire last week . . . "

Kerr ceased to listen. Even to his untutored eyes, this fire had been one of unusual severity. Then he remembered something that should have been very obvious: spirits burned. But what had the thief been doing or carrying to start the fire? Thieves no longer went around with dark lanterns which could fall over: they didn't light up a cigarette and carelessly throw the match into a pile of combustible material.

He crossed the cellar to where the station officer now stood, by the ladder. "Have you any ideas on how this fire started?"

The station officer shook his head. "Once it got going, obviously the spirit fed it, but as to what started it . . . Would you like someone to come along from H.Q.?"

"The request will have to come from my D.I., but he's certain to make it."

"So you're wondering if it was arson?"

"I'm just wondering at the moment. For instance, once the fire got going, what caught this bloke and stopped him climbing out?"

"He could've panicked? Or got temporarily knocked out by something?"

"Such as what?"

"Luckily, that's your problem."

"That's for sure," answered Kerr. "Have you finished here?"

"I'll keep a pump standing by for a while, but all my blokes can clear out of the cellar if that's what you want?"

"It would be best." Kerr mentally checked that he had taken all necessary preliminary steps because if he hadn't Fusil would very soon point out the fact. He watched the firemen climb the ladder, then stared up through the burned-out hole at the ceiling of the shop. What a terrible thing was a fire in a wine shop, he thought: all that booze just going up in flames. He could have done with some of the bubbly for an engagement party.

Fusil held the telephone receiver to his ear with his left hand and tapped impatiently on the desk with his right. "Yes, sir, I know ... "

Kywood, detective chief inspector, interrupted him. "Bob, it's a big job. That's fact." The telephone slightly distorted his voice and gave it a whining quality not otherwise apparent.

"I realise that, of course ... "

"And it was pulled inside the boundaries."

There was no arguing round that one, thought Fusil resentfully. The Jack of Hearts café was just a hundred yards inside the Fortrow borough boundaries: if only the villains had pulled the job sooner, the investigations would have been the county C.I.D.'s pigeon, not his.

"It's the fourth hi-jacking in the past

two years, so people are getting worried." Kywood's voice became warmer. "The other three were in county territory and no one ever got anywhere in solving 'em so this gives us a real chance to show 'em. I'm betting you'll nail the villains well and truly and show the county boys what we're made of."

Any moment now, thought Fusil, he'd call for three cheers.

"The first thing, of course, is to concentrate on tracing where and how they flog the whisky. Don't forget it's all export stuff."

"D'you know if that means it's a different proof?"

"I wouldn't know, Bob. You'll be able to find that out, won't you? Now I don't mind telling you, I'm relying on you and your blokes really pulling out your fingers." Kywood rang off.

Fusil replaced the receiver, stood up, yawned, and stretched. The stolen whisky was the kind of a bitch of a case that no ambitious D.I. welcomed. The hi-jacking had probably been carried out by a London mob who took the whisky straight up to London and their only contact with Fortrow was the site of the actual theft. The chances of the borough C.I.D. latching on to anything of significance were slim to the point of nonexistent, but because the robbery had taken place within the borough boundaries, it would appear on his crime sheets. If it remained unsolved, the finger would be pointed at him.

He took his pipe from his pocket, filled it with tobacco, and lit it. He was hungry for promotion and hated anything or anyone who might get in the way of it. His fellow D.I.s might see themselves ending their careers, if they were very lucky, as detective superintendents, but he wanted to make assistant chief constable and if he didn't do so he would count himself a failure. He was a sufficient realist to know the odds against him. Apart from anything else, he was too sharp for his own good, as witness the Burchell case when he'd pursued criminals beyond the permitted boundaries and had been found out: one of these days he might go that little bit further which would spell disaster.

The telephone rang. It was Kerr. The dead man appeared to have broken into the cellar by forcing the grating of a window. Should an expert from the fire brigade be called to give his opinion on the cause of the fire? What about contacting the police photographer?

After answering Kerr and ringing off, Fusil telephoned the coroner's officer, reported the facts, and said there would have to be a P.M. He then contacted the pathologist, said the police doctor had been called, and tried tactfully to express the hope that the pathologist would get out to the wine store before too long. The pathologist curtly answered that he'd get there when he could and not before.

Fusil's pipe had gone out and he re-lit it. He left and went into the next room, Braddon's, to find the detective sergeant was out. He wrote a note and left it on the desk to tell Braddon where he was going and to ask Braddon to speak to county H.Q. and ask the C.R.O. whether any useful facts had come to light from the previous whisky hi-jackings. He hesitated, then added a further request to contact the C.R.O. at New Scotland Yard and ask them for any help they could give. County H.Q. should have done this, but he did not have much faith in their lines of communication.

3

WAKELY, from the fire department, was a middle-aged man who had the appearance of one who'd met more than his fair share of suffering: there was a withdrawn expression in his eyes, and he often looked as if he'd suddenly lost himself in memories. He stood in the cellar of the wine shop and spoke to Fusil in his low, pedantic voice. "Once the spirits caught, they obviously fed the fire and stoked it up to the intensity it reached. What isn't obvious is what started the fire in the first place."

"Could a small fire set the whole thing in motion?"

"It doesn't seem very likely. The bottles were in wire racks round the walls, the walls are brick, the floor is stone. The only wood was in the roof and the chute. Unless there was a pile of old rubbish down here . . . ?" He looked at the D.I.

Fusil shook his head. "We've had a word with the manager who swears he kept the cellars spick and span. According to him, there wasn't a single scrap of loose paper around."

"Then it brings us back to the problem of the initial fire." Wakely gestured at some of the rubble. "I did think I caught the smell of paraffin in one piece of charred wood, but I couldn't detect the taste of paraffin when I used a bit of bread. I'd send several bits of wood from various parts of this cellar to the laboratories and see if they can tell you anything about them."

"I'll certainly do that."

"By the way, there's something interesting over here." Wakely stepped across to a conical pile of rubble and bent down to point beneath a shattered bean. "That worm-like thing is the remains of a candle wick."

Fusil squatted on his heels and saw the charred remains which were about two inches long and coloured grey.

Wakely spoke still more pedantically. "It's an odd fact that if a candle is consumed all at once the wick often gets preserved because the supporting stalk skeleton makes it relatively tough."

Fusil stared at the wick. A candle was a favourite tool of the arsonist since it provided a time fuse. But he remembered an advertisement he had often seen of a man judging the quality of a wine or sherry by holding the glass in front of a candle. Did that sort of thing really go on in the cellars of a wine shop which was one of a chain — if anyone did judge drink like this, wouldn't it be done at head office, not in one of the branches: He stood up. "What's your general impression of things?"

"With nothing definite to go on, I'd say the fire was deliberately set."

"Are you likely to be able to be more specific?"

Wakely shrugged his shoulders. "It's impossible to say at this stage."

Fusil stared round again at the debris. It would all have to be sifted as carefully as possible and that would require several men — who would mostly have to come from the uniformed branch. The duty inspector was going to moan like hell.

A P.C. called down from the floor above. "Detective inspector, sir."

"Yes?"

"Message from the station. Will you please contact the detective sergeant on the pocket radio."

"Have you got a W.T. set?"

"Yes, sir."

"Hang on up there for me, then." Fusil turned and called Kerr over. "See that there, under the beam? It's a charred wick. Lift it very carefully — after it's been photographed — and get it into a tube. And see it's wedged with cotton wool and the tube's kept horizontal."

Kerr nodded.

"When you've done that, cut along to the house where the manager of this place is staying and see what he can tell us."

Fusil left the cellar and climbed up the ladder. He called the P.C. over to the counter, on which the till was ironically recording 'No Sale'. "Let's have your set." The P.C. handed him the pocket radio and he switched it on, called up the station, and asked to speak to Braddon. Braddon told him that the hi-jacked lorry had just been discovered in the hills above the chest hospital. Fusil said he'd get over there and asked for explicit directions,

31

which he was given.

Would the pathologist turn up soon? wondered Fusil. Or had he time to get out to the lorry and have a quick look around: He decided to risk the other's wrath, should he arrive early, and drive over to the lorry at once.

A P.C. motor cyclist, from traffic division, was guarding the lorry. "I was sent here by H.Q., sir. They had a call from the owner of the woods, who found the lorry. I checked the number with Records and they said it had just been put on the latest list of stolen vehicles."

Fusil looked round. The clearing in the woods was oval in shape and about fifty feet at the widest point. The ground was covered in wild grass but for no readily discernible reason the wild growing brambles, bracken, and rose-bay willow herb, did not start until close to the edge of the clearing. The lorry was parked over to the right and its track through the grass was still visible if looked at obliquely. He knelt down and checked the ground. Although the grass was wet from the recent rain, now stopped, the ground was still rock hard so that the chances of any worthwhile impressions were virtually nil. He went across to the lorry and opened the off-side cab door, using his handkerchief to prevent the smudging of any prints. There were some papers and the log book of hours in one of the two compartments and some scrumpled up paper on the floor, but otherwise he could see nothing. He was hardly surprised. Modern villains had learned the vital necessity of leaving no traces behind, not even a thread of cotton from a coat.

Men would have to be drafted up here, he thought, to search every inch of the ground in case something of importance was lying about. That meant more P.C.s — the duty inspector would do his nut and probably there'd be a first-class row. The police photographer must come here after he'd finished at Verlay's Wine Store. Braddon would have to take charge of things because he, Fusil, must concentrate on the case involving the dead man — potentially the more important case because the reason for the man's being burned to death had not yet been ascertained.

As he stood in the centre of the clearing,

to the side of the lorry, sunlight came through a small patch of blue sky and it picked out the sharp lines of determination in his face, lines which sometimes made him falsely appear stern in an unthinking, harsh manner. There was no surplus flesh on his face or body, such as often burdened men in their early middle age, yet he certainly did not look younger than he was. He lived and worked too intensely for the years not to mark him. He spoke to the P.C. "Hang on here until Sergeant Braddon arrives."

"I'm due back at H.Q. in fifteen minutes' time, sir."

"Then you'll be late, won't you?"

He left the clearing and walked back down the track to his car. He called up county H.Q. on the radio and asked them to contact eastern division H.Q. by telephone and tell Braddon to come straight away to the lorry to start investigations.

When the call was over, Fusil sat back in the driving seat and just for a few moments relaxed. The view spread out before him was an attractive one. To the west was a typical patch-work of green countryside, partly in sunshine now, which contained fields of every shape and size and several small villages. To the south was Fortrow and beyond the sea, somewhat hazy so that horizon and sky melted inconclusively into each other. There was beauty, peace, and a sense of continuity here — a far cry from his work. Some of his fellow policemen, he knew, thought him to be a man without emotions, shocked by nothing, unmoved by distress, incapable of appreciating any beauty. They failed to understand how single-minded he was when trying to bring to justice a criminal: he could appreciate things just as well as they, but he would not normally give up the time to do so.

He took out his pipe from his pocket, lowered the window, and tapped out the ash, filled it, and lit it. Why did man everywhere do so much to try to destroy the peace and beauty which surrounded him? A naive question? Not if one had ever had to tell a woman that her husband had just been killed, or a father that his daughter had been attacked and raped.

Kerr, in the cellar of Verlay's Wine Store,

was no longer bothered by the dead man. The blackened corpse, arm and leg raised, teeth shamming a grin in that ruined face, was just part of the debris.

He had carried down a chair and he stood on this to examine, with the aid of a torch, the iron bars which had been forced. He moved the beam of the torch up and down, to alter the angle at which it struck the metal, and he saw an impression on the left-hand bar. Then, almost immediately, he saw another impression below the first. One had a curved edge, the other a straight one with, in the centre, a small V indented. Assuming the bars had been forced apart with an hydraulic jack, it was reasonable to assume that those marks had been caused by the base of the jack. He took a notebook from his pocket and made a sketch of the impressions.

He climbed down from the chair and looked up through the hole in the ceiling at the uniformed P.C. above. "Isn't there any sign of anyone yet?"

"Not a sausage, mate."

"What the hell are they all doing?"

"Resting. It's only the erks and narks

like you and me what have to work."

"You do what?" asked Kerr jeeringly. "You blokes in blue don't know what work is — clocking on and off just like an office job."

"Don't you start shouting that one at me! I've got a sergeant to see I'm doing what I ought to be when I'm on duty, but you blokes just slope off and have a couple of hours in the flics watching a Scandinavian film."

Kerr chuckled. "Talking about them, did you read about the latest?"

"Is it hot stuff?" asked the P.C. with great interest.

"They say that if you've got a weak heart, you'd better stay away."

"What's it called?"

"You wouldn't be eager, would you? What's the matter? Won't that blonde of yours play the right games?"

"My . . . " began the P.C., but stopped abruptly.

Kerr was about to make a ribald comment when he saw the reason for the P.C.'s silence — the pathologist.

The pathologist, dressed in a very smart pin-striped suit, stood by the ladder and looked down. He examined Kerr with an expression that could have been distaste, then studied the body. There was a man, thought Kerr rudely, who wouldn't know what to do with a blonde on a deserted tropical beach.

The pathologist moved out of sight. Kerr heard him giving peremptory orders to his secretary to pass over boots, gloves, and overalls. Soon after the last of the stream of orders, he climbed down the ladder, followed by his secretary, an elderly man who was remarkably agile for his age.

"Where's the detective inspector?" asked the pathologist.

"He got called away to another case, sir."

"That's no excuse for his not being here when I arrive."

You two argue that one out, thought Kerr cheerfully.

There was a clump of feet from above and the lugubrious face of Detective Sergeant Walsh peered down. "Are you ready?" he asked.

"Always ready, always willing," answered Kerr.

Walsh muttered something and then climbed down the ladder with some of his photographic equipment. When he reached the floor, he shouted at the P.C. above to pass him down the rest.

"Sarge," said Kerr, "there are some impressions on the bent bar at the window which must be photographed."

"All right, all right, just give me a chance to breathe. Rush, rush, rush!" Walsh carefully put down the tripod at a point where the debris was not too thick. He used a handkerchief to mop his brow. "It's hot and stuffy here," he muttered.

"I'll get some air-conditioning laid on next time."

The pathologist spoke sharply. "Have you come here to chatter or to work? Photograph the body from over there — and there — and there," he ordered, stabbing the air with his forefinger. "And will someone please tell me where the detective inspector is?"

Walsh took the photographs and then stepped back. The pathologist moved forward and began to examine the head of the dead man, working with the delicate touch of a surgeon.

Fusil came down the ladder.

The pathologist looked up briefly. "Very kind of you to honour us with your presence," he said.

Fusil's expression tightened. He crossed to Kerr. "Have you questioned the manager and his wife?"

"Not yet, sir. I've been waiting here . . . "

"That's half your trouble — you're always waiting. Get on and do some work."

"It seemed to me . . . "

"Stop arguing."

Kerr turned and crossed to the ladder, which he climbed. The world was a very unjust place. Still, he'd survive. He went to his car, suddenly remembered the wick of the candle, and returned to tell Walsh to photograph it and detail someone to pack it in a container.

The address to which the manager and his wife had gone was in Farnleigh. Kerr arrived at one o'clock and, mindful of public relations, decided not to interrupt the Jarvises at what might well be their meal time. He was also hungry. He had a sandwich lunch and a pint and then drove on to Kirwood Avenue.

The door of number 34 was opened by a woman in her early twenties who looked thoroughly harassed — sudden shrieks and yells from at least two children explained why. He introduced himself and asked if he could see Mr. Jarvis and she showed him into the front room — a brightly decorated and furnished room that was immediately attractive.

Mr. Jarvis was a tall, thin man, approaching the end of middle age, with a nervous, jerky manner of speaking. "Look — my wife's proper shocked. Terrible sort of thing to happen. Unless you just have to speak to her . . . "

"I'm sure you can tell me all I need to know, Mr. Jarvis," replied Kerr. "What I want to clear up first of all is what was down in the cellar that would burn? You know the kind of stuff — wood, paper, old sacks?"

"I used to keep the cellar very tidy. There was not even any wooden or cardboard boxes — always took them out right away, I did. When Mr. Ball from head office came around, he was always saying what a tidy cellar I kept." He spoke with a pride that seemed pathetic.

"Then you can't suggest what could have started the fire?"

"There wasn't anything. I was always most particular about fire risk. The man what broke in did the fire." Jarvis' voice rose. "Who was he? What was he doing in my cellar? He could've had us burned to death. My wife's frightened sick."

Kerr murmured a few words of sympathy, only too aware that no words of his would bring any comfort. The Jarvises were clearly experiencing the retrospective fear that so often afflicted people after a crime in which they had not been directly injured: for some time, their minds would haunt them with all the terrors they might have suffered. "Have you any idea who the man in the cellar might be?"

Jarvis shook his head. "How could I know that? I didn't know nothing until my wife shook me awake. If she hadn't woken me up, we could've both been burned to death."

"You haven't received any threats from anyone?"

"Why should I receive threats?" he asked plaintively.

"The old protection racket — fork over

a hundred quid or we burn your place down."

"If anything like that ever happened, I'd have told the police immediately."

Kerr turned over a page in his notebook. "What kind of stock did you have in the place?"

"The same as usual. We never carry extra except for Christmas." Jarvis began to speak more easily. "It's a very regular trade, you understand, except when the government shoves on new taxes. In any case, I always keep a very close check and it's my boast that I've never been caught short of stock. Head office has never had cause to complain." His expression suddenly crumpled.

"What's up?" asked Kerr, astonished by the abrupt change.

"It's . . . it's the future. Got me worried, it has. Head office has shut down two branches in the last year on account of competition from cut-price stores. The managers were made redundant. I'm getting on a bit. If they was to decide not to rebuild . . . " He looked a very frightened man.

"They'll rebuild, twice the size of before,"

said Kerr, with false certainty.

Jarvis shook his head. "The firm's old-fashioned and doesn't like new ideas. I told 'em to drop their prices to meet the competition from the cut-price places, but they wouldn't ... Said their customers wanted the old kind of service. Customers these days want everything cheap. Things aren't what they used to be."

They never were, thought Kerr, and a good job too. In the old days, the average copper was hard put to find the price of half a pint.

Detective Sergeant Braddon organised the search of the clearing in the woods with his usual efficiency. This was routine work and he had always been good at that, having the necessary kind of patient mind. What he lacked was ambition and imagination, but he knew he lacked these qualities and yet didn't give a damn. When he retired, he'd settle down into the kind of life he'd always wanted: a little gardening, a little walking, and a lot of sitting about with nothing much to do.

He called across to one of the two P.C.s who was using a stick to search the thick

44

undergrowth beyond the lorry and he told the other to do a better job. The P.C.'s lips moved, but Braddon heard nothing. The fact that he'd just been cursed failed to worry him in the slightest. All P.C.s had always cursed their sergeants.

The dog handler, dog on a short lead, came up to where he stood. "There's nothing, Sarge."

"Are you sure you've covered everywhere?"

"Alex has been over everything and everywhere a dozen times."

Braddon stared down at the panting dog. "Looks like we've got an empty plot, then."

"Nothing in the lorry?"

"Nothing and Dabs says it's empty of prints except those which must be the driver's."

"It's a slick job."

"That's for sure."

"What was the whisky worth?"

"Something like ten thousand quid at shop prices."

The dog handler whistled.

Braddon used his handkerchief to wipe the sweat from his brow. Since the rain had stopped, the day had become very sultry.

"Did you cover the woods between here and the road?"

"I told you, Sarge, Alex has been everywhere. There ain't any traces."

Braddon sighed. Villains were getting too flaming clever.

4

ROWAN looked at his watch: the time was nearly five-thirty. Was he going to be able to get away at a reasonable hour? Heather had suggested they went to the pictures tonight and he'd promised to take her. He daren't let her down because it was the first time she'd asked him to take her out for weeks: the first time, in fact, since their last row which had been so bitter that for a while it had seemed they must finally separate. It was strange. Until that moment, he had been able to imagine their separation with equanimity, certain it was he who, from the beginning, had been in the right: but when they'd looked at each other with hate and despair and had realised everything was almost over, they'd suddenly both been swept by a terrible sense of impending loss and hurt. They'd tried everything they could to patch things up and seemed to have succeeded, but he sensed the patching was still thin: it wouldn't need much to upset everything once more.

He walked up the street and went into the cut-price liquor store run by Sharman & Co., Ltd. Bottles were stored in open shelves and customers entered, picked up a wire basket, went down the left-hand gangway and came back up the right-hand one to the till and the exit door. The woman behind the till was knitting. When he introduced himself, she exclaimed with surprise and put the knitting down by the till.

"We're trying to trace some whisky that's just been stolen," he explained.

She spoke sharply. "You won't find any here."

He smiled and for a moment his expression of general discontent was banished. "I'm not suggesting we will. What I'm after finding is whether anyone's approached you trying to sell whisky on the cheap?"

"All our supplies come from the wholesalers who own the shop."

"D'you never get any travellers?"

"No. They visit the warehouse, not here."

A middle-aged, smartly dressed, retired-colonel-type man came in, picked up a wire basket, went straight to the gin, put four bottles in the basket, and paid with a ten-pound note.

Rowan watched him leave with envious dislike. Nobody could try to tell Rowan that money wasn't all important in life. If he'd had enough money to give Heather the kind of life she'd wanted, she wouldn't have gone modelling and then he wouldn't have spent so many agonising hours wondering whether she did something more than model.

"Is there anything else?" demanded the woman.

He jerked his thoughts back to the present. "D'you sell MacLaren Highland Whisky?"

"It's up there, on the shelves."

He went back to the whisky shelves. There were over two dozen bottles of MacLaren whisky in one compartment, priced at a shilling a bottle less than other brands. The label was one made familiar by extensive T.V. advertising: there was a poetic scene from the Mull of Kintyre and in the foreground was a stag. Under the stag ran the motto: 'The malt whisky the connoisseurs have discovered'. Rowan picked up one of the bottles. Fusil said the stolen whisky had 'Export' printed across the right-hand corner of the label and three numbers punched in the left-hand corner: this label was unmarked, as were all the others in the rack. He took the bottle to the counter and paid for it.

"D'you find this whisky is popular?" he asked.

"People are drinking it more and more." Her manner became less frosty. "My husband won't touch the ordinary grain whiskies these days — and they're a little bit more expensive."

This bottle was for Fusil. He was tempted to buy another for Heather, but knew he couldn't really afford to.

He left the shop and stood to the side of the pavement as he wrote the name of the shop on the label of the bottle. Instead of selling it to the canteen to recoup the cost, Fusil would probably fiddle it for himself. Rank always won. He took the list from his pocket and checked the address of the next drink shop he had to visit, then cut back through a side street to the High Street at a point above the cattle market — which, since it was Tuesday, was open and causing endless traffic jams. Findren and Sons was very old-fashioned in style with a long, mahogany counter, two assistants who wore dark coats, and only a few bottles in sight. The firm was widely noted for the quality of its wines and because its trade was with the wealthier and it still offered considerable credit, its sales had not really been affected by the cut-price stores or the wine clubs. Practically all the good hotels and restaurants in and around Fortrow bought their wines from Findren.

Rowan spoke to the tall and thin assistant — his companion was short and fat — and said he was trying to discover whether anyone was offering stolen whisky for sale.

"We do not," said the tall and thin assistant, "indulge in that sort of trade." His tone of voice suggested he would not be astonished to hear that other, much lesser stores, did.

"No one's come in and sounded you out on buying any MacLaren whisky?"

"Certainly not."

"D'you sell much of it?"

"More and more," said the short and fat man, speaking for the first time.

The tall and thin man sniffed. He spoke in a patronising voice. "People are very simple. They actually believe the advertisements on telly. As if drinking MacLaren whisky could begin to make anyone a connoisseur! Another thing, it's not a pure malt whisky, but a blended one like all the others, only it has a shade less grain whisky. Still, the average whisky drinker hasn't any palate."

The manager hurried out of his office to discover what all the talking was about. He was an over-neat, fussy little man whose manner became peremptory as soon as he had a good look at Rowan and noted the quality of his clothes. "Well — what's the trouble?"

The tall assistant answered. "He's a detective, Mr. Pills, and wants to know if we've bought any stolen whisky."

"Of course not," snapped the manager. "I would have thought that was obvious to anyone of even average intelligence." He stalked back to his office.

Rowan bought a bottle of MacLaren whisky and left. If ever he won the pools and could afford to drink, he'd go to hell before he bought so much as a bottle of soda water from Findren and Sons.

Kerr drove up the centre road that ran through the large industrial estate to the north-west of Fortrow which was on land that six years before had been green fields. A notice directed him down a side road and this brought him to the warehouse which, set behind a ten-foot-high chain-link fence, was rectangular in shape, brick built, and had a thick concrete roof. There were no windows and the doors were of metal with special heavy-duty locks. Immediately to the right of the warehouse was an office, a separate low, wooden building. Kerr parked the Hillman in the road, walked past an Aston Martin that filled him with covetous greed, and went through to the office building which consisted of a front reception area and a single room beyond. He rang the bell on the counter and waited. The reception area was sparsely furnished and purely functional. There was the counter, a small table on which was a telephone that was linked to two extensions and a typewriter, a rush mat on the wooden floor, two uncomfortable wooden chairs, and a pictureless calendar on the near wall.

A woman came out of the office. She was in her middle twenties and Kerr's automatic reaction was to whistle silently. A blonde, very pretty, with a body that did all the right things at the right places, she wore a dress that looked as if it had been moulded to her. If he weren't an engaged man, he'd nominate her as one of the people he'd most like to be shipwrecked with.

"Can I do something for you?" she asked.

That was a leading question! There wasn't much she couldn't do for him. "I'm from the borough C.I.D. Detective Constable Kerr." Her dress was fashionably short. Her legs, visible over the top of the counter, were very shapely. If he weren't an engaged man, he'd really appreciate them. "I'd like a word with Mr. Sharman, if that's possible?"

"You want to see my husband?" She smiled. "What's he been up to now?"

He smiled back. "Nothing that I know of. I'm only here for some information."

She rested her elbows on the counter. Her dress had an interesting divide and

Kerr automatically checked on how interesting it became when she leaned forward, before he remembered and jerked his gaze away.

"My husband's in the warehouse. I'll give him a ring. There's one thing — he never objects to stopping work to talk!" She stood upright, turned, and pressed one of the bars at the base of the telephone to call an extension.

She was a lulu, no mucking around on that score, thought Kerr. And from the way she had smiled at him and leaned over, careless about the front of her dress . . . Physical attraction was the most devastating of emotions. Married and reasonably happy, everything had gone smoothly until there stepped into her life a curly-headed, good-looking, carefree man, tough yet in no way brutal, who set alight the wild passions in her. Irresistibly swept onwards, tormented by her desires, she struggled to resist him and could not. She demanded a meeting. Seconds after they met, she kissed him with a volcanic . . .

"He'll be here in a minute," she said.

It was a good thing, thought Kerr a trifle guiltily, that Helen didn't have a private line to his thoughts. He comforted his conscience. If Mrs. Sharman were twice as passionate as Cleopatra, he wouldn't be interested.

The outer door opened and a man came into the reception area. He was large and heavy, in the region of fifteen stone, but was in no way gross: he moved with the casual ease of someone in first-class physical condition. He had a round, even face, a neat mouth, a ready smile, and a square, strong chin. Although dressed in dirtied green overalls and open shirt, there was no mistaking his position of authority. "I gather you're from the police?" he said, in a deep, baritone voice.

"Detective Constable Kerr, sir."

"Glad to meet you." Sharman shook hands with a grip so firm that Kerr had to exercise considerable pressure to counter it. "What's the panic, then?" He sat down on the edge of the counter, took a silver cigar case from the pocket of his overalls, and offered it. "D'you use these?"

Kerr momentarily hesitated, then accepted one. It was not very often the chance came his way.

"D'you prefer to pierce or cut the end?" asked Sharman.

"I don't mind," replied Kerr, a shade uneasy at being presented with a problem that was beyond him.

"I always cut — seems better. Borrow my cutter."

There was something about Sharman's tone of voice which worried Kerr, but when he took the cutter the other's expression was merely one of good humour.

Mrs. Sharman said she must get on with the work and returned to the inside office. It was only after the door shut that Kerr realised how closely he'd watched her.

Sharman said: "Can't beat Havana leaf, can you? Nothing else comes so smooth."

He'd smoked so few cigars, thought Kerr, he wouldn't know whether this one came from Havana or Timbuktu.

"However," said Sharman, "I'm sure you haven't come here to discuss the merits or demerits of cigars?"

Once again, Kerr thought he noticed an odd note to the other's voice, yet once again Sharman's expression remained blandly good-humoured. "We're trying," said Kerr, "to trace some stolen whisky and wondered whether anyone had been along to offer you some cheaply?"

Sharman shook his head. "No one. In any case, we only buy from wholesalers, distillers, or importers. Is this on account of the whisky robbery?"

"That's right."

"And you think the thieves would already have been trying to sell the whisky?" Sharman suddenly laughed. "Still, that's trying to teach my grandmother to suck eggs. Now why suck eggs? Why should anyone want to suck an egg?"

"I've no idea," muttered Kerr. "D'you handle a lot of MacLaren whisky?"

"We do. Thanks to the T.V. advertising campaign, it's become really popular. I'll tell you something." Sharman drew on his cigar, then exhaled slowly, savouring the smoke. "When we started here from nothing, my wife and me, we shopped around for who'd give us the best credit — needed credit, we did. MacLaren offered two months and better terms for bulk ordering than anyone else. It wasn't all that popular, then, but the T.V. advertising had started and I'd a feeling. So I took a gamble and stocked up. Best thing I ever did. We're now selling over forty thousand bottles a year and that's still rising. Represents a turnover, that does. It's big money — for a man in a very small way of business like me," he ended.

Small way of business, hell! thought Kerr. An Aston Martin and a wife who dressed like a million and looked the hottest thing since chilli con carne — nothing small there.

Sharman spoke in an off-handed manner. "There seem to have been quite a few whisky thefts recently?"

"This is the fourth in two years," replied Kerr reluctantly.

"Someone's making some profit, then. And you're not doing too well at catching them?"

"It always takes time," said Kerr quickly.

"Of course." Sharman slipped off the counter and patted Kerr familiarly on the shoulder. "I'm sure you and everyone else is doing everything possible to catch the thieves. You'd better succeed, you know, or businessmen like me will see crime does pay and we'll have a stab at it." He laughed loudly.

People often seemed to think crime

was funny, thought Kerr sourly. That was unless and until they became caught up in it.

Sharman jabbed the air with his cigar. "Well, glad to help you. Any time, just come and ask." He shook hands forcefully, then left.

Feeling disgruntled, but not yet certain why, Kerr returned to the car. He drew on the cigar, inhaled, and coughed violently. Camel, not Havana, he thought with uncharacteristic spitefulness. He suddenly realised why he felt disgruntled. Sharman had ended the interview rather as if he were an elderly schoolmaster dismissing a very young schoolboy.

Fusil was inside Verlay's Wine Store when he was called to the courtyard at the rear. A uniformed P.C. pointed behind a wooden tub in which grew a tired-looking shrub. "There's a car jack behind there, sir."

Fusil peered round the shrub and visually examined the jack and the long handle by its side. "Why the hell wasn't this found earlier?"

"Couldn't say, sir," answered the P.C. stolidly.

"Tell whoever made the search to report to me." Fusil studied the jack as well as he could. It lay on its side with the base towards him: the base was an eighth of an inch thick, semi-circular at the top, straight at the bottom, and along the bottom a piece of metal had been nicked out. Without a doubt, this jack matched the marks on the bar across the cellar window.

When there was only a single item to be photographed and the quality of the print would be relatively unimportant, someone from the station took the photo rather than calling Walsh down from county H.Q. Fusil gave orders for the jack to be photographed in position, then to be removed for finger-print testing. He returned to the shop, walked forward to the jagged hole in the floor, and looked below. The extremities of the body had been tied up in plastic bags and two assistants from an undertaker's firm were gently easing the body on to a plastic sheet which would then be put on a stretcher and hoisted up.

Fusil put his pipe in his mouth but did not light up. If this fire had been deliberately started, why? An insurance swindle, the protection-racket, straight revenge, a fire to cover up theft, pyromania? Enquiries would have to be made into what sort of insurance cover there was on the place, but it was difficult to imagine that the well-known company which owned this store and many others in the south had set up in the swindling business. The protection racket? There'd been no reports of any movements in this field and surely he'd have received some before a shop was actually fired? Theft? How could the theft be concealed when the iron bars were bent? Pyromania — pyromaniacs usually chose much easier targets.

Could there be any connection between this fire and the theft of the whisky, other than the tenuous one that both concerned liquor?

He left the shattered building and pushed past some sightseers. As he climbed into his car, a local reporter tried to question him, but he gave the time of the press conference and then slammed the door and drove off.

Once back at the station, he sat down at the desk in his office, yawned, took off his coat, and wondered whether he ought to ring Josephine to warn her he might be pretty late back home?

Welland came into the room, radiating boisterous good cheer. Fusil trusted him to do most routine work, but tried to avoid sending him out on a job which demanded too much intelligence and imagination.

"H.Q. was on the blower, sir, with the dope from the C.R.O. I've made notes." He passed across a foolscap page of typing.

As always, Welland's typing contained a large number of mis-hit keys, but it was readable. Little was known about the whisky thefts. It was obvious that professionals had carried out the hi-jackings, but no word had come through on who they might be or how the stolen whisky was being disposed of. Fusil looked up. "Did Records add anything to this over the 'phone?"

"No, sir."

Welland left. Wearily, Fusil picked up the latest crime reports from this desk: two cars stolen, a fight down by the docks, broached cargo at Elwick Dock, a mugged Japanese sailor, an attempted hold-up at a bank in Ribstowe. He sighed. There was little time available to investigate much of the less serious crime, but today's big

63

villain was yesterday's little villain who'd decided crime did pay. Both divisions of the Fortrow C.I.D. needed more men to operate really efficiently, but there were not the funds available. Undoubtedly, it would have been a good thing for the borough force to have been merged into the county force, as the county force had for a long time wanted, but the local citizens still fought the merger — on the grounds of pride, not police efficiency.

Braddon came into the room. Fusil began to scrape out the bowl of his pipe. "Well — what's the news?"

"Practically no joy at all, sir."

Fusil's voice sharpened. "Hell, there must be something."

"Everywhere was searched over and over, I had a dog working a couple of hours, and Dabs checked that lorry as if he was looking for gold dust."

Fusil swore.

Braddon spoke lugubriously. "How's the fire look, sir?"

"It's a mess." He tapped out his pipe into the half-filled ash-tray, then pushed across the latest crime reports. "These have just come in. We'll have to check what we can, but don't waste much time on them we've too much on our plate."

Braddon picked up the crime reports and read quickly through them.

Fusil leaned back in his chair until it was resting against the wall. "Pete — if you'd nicked ten thousand quid's worth of whisky, how would you go about flogging it?"

"I'd take it straight up to London."

It was the obvious answer, thought Fusil. Up there, ten thousand pounds' worth of stolen whisky was nothing: pubs could buy a few bottles each and never be found out and there were so many of them that they could take the whole consignment. "We may learn something from a grasser, but nothing's looking too hopeful at the moment."

Things, thought Braddon, seldom did look hopeful. He gained some comfort from that fact.

Kerr reported to Fusil as the D.I. was preparing to leave for home. "I saw Sharman, sir: tried to report earlier but you weren't in. Sharman says he hasn't been approached by anyone over cheap whisky and in any case he only buys from distillers, wholesalers, or importers. His yearly turn-over of MacLaren whisky is around forty thousand bottles."

"That sounds a hell of a lot of whisky. All right, thanks." Fusil shuffled some papers together, then realised Kerr was not moving. "Is there something more?"

"In a way, yes, sir."

"In what way?"

"Well, it's very difficult to put a name to it."

"Can you, or can't you? If you can, get on with it."

"It's just . . . Well, Sharman's manner." Kerr spoke with very unusual diffidence. "He seemed . . . He seemed to be laughing at me part of the time."

"Is that so very surprising?" asked Fusil, with mild sarcasm. "What kind of laughing?"

Kerr spoke in a rush. "It may be a load of old cod's wallop, but it seemed he was secretly jeering at me."

Kerr waited a moment, but when no more was said, he left. Fusil picked up a pencil and played with it. Kerr was intelligent and perceptive of others' emotions, but it was so easy to be mistaken. In any case, perhaps he'd acted in his most slap-happy manner and Sharman, known in Fortrow as a very shrewd businessman, had found him extremely gauche.

Helen met Kerr in the hall of her parents' home and kissed him quickly. She was not beautiful by conventional standards, yet the warmth in her eyes when she looked at him gave her a very special kind of beauty. "Well, darling," she said softly, "what's it like to have been engaged for a whole twenty-four hours?"

"I haven't really given it a thought."

"You what?" Then she saw his grin. "Pig! Just for that, you can have bread and butter for supper, and nothing more."

He spoke hastily. "I promise you I woke up singing, I've been singing all day, and I've been so happy that the sight of old Bob Fusil looking like Methuselah with the toothache hasn't meant a thing."

She kissed him again. "Just think, before too long we'll have our own place and when you come home it'll be just you and me." She linked her arm with his. "It's so odd, John, the idea of us living together. One moment I have to remind myself it's really going to happen, the next I can't think why we aren't already doing it."

"Nor can I!"

She giggled. "You've got a one-track mind, darling."

"Try walking down it — it's a hell of an interesting track."

"Norah said how terribly sexy you looked."

"Who's she?"

"You know perfectly well. That friend of mine with red hair."

"Her! She's no beginner."

"John, take that wolfish expression off your face. As from last night, you don't have such thoughts."

"No, ma'am."

There was the sound of a door being opened as noisily as possible, a heavy cough, and then Mr. Barley stepped out into the hall. " 'Evening, John. Come on in and have a beer."

Helen and Kerr went into the front room. Mrs. Barley was sitting down, but she got up and kissed him on both cheeks and fussed over him as if he were her own son returned after a long time away from home.

Fusil stared at the empty fireplace in the sitting-room and ignored the T.V., even though it was showing a current affairs programme that usually interested him. "Bob," said Josephine. He looked up. "Why not go to bed? You look so tired and you're not watching the programme."

"I was thinking."

She put down the stitching she had been doing. "Do you have to work so hard?" she asked softly. "Are you certain you couldn't delegate some of your work?" She spoke more quickly. "You can't do everything yourself, Bob."

He smiled briefly. "What are you really saying? That I'm not nearly so indispensable as I'd like to think myself?"

"You're quite indispensable to me and that's why I get concerned."

He reached over and took her hand. "Don't worry, Jo, thinking never killed anyone."

"What's the trouble?"

He sighed as he released her. "This fourth hi-jacking of whisky. Each hi-jacking has been of MacLaren whisky and on the face of it that suggests a leakage up north at the distillery. But

69

the reports on previous hi-jackings make it clear that the most extensive enquiries at the distillery turned up nothing." He took the pipe from his pocket and rubbed the bowl against the palm of his left hand. "I've been working on the theory that a fourth set of enquiries up there won't do any better. I've an idea."

"What's that?"

"It's based on the fact that a hell of a lot of loads of MacLaren whisky have come south of London in the past two years, a number of them bigger than the ones that have been pinched. If the leak was at the distillery, I'd expect the thefts to be of the largest loads. Therefore, I think the leak is down here, in Fortrow. I've made a quick check and the fact the whisky is labelled export doesn't necessarily mean it's cargo being exported. It can be whisky going aboard a ship as part of the ship's stores for passenger consumption. The information of a coming load could be fed to the villains by someone aboard who knows when it's due."

"How will you find out if that's how they're doing it?"

"List the ships that were in port for the

other thefts and the ones in port now: if there's a ship that turns up each time, things will begin to look interesting."

She folded up her sewing. "Sometimes, Bob, you frighten me a little."

"Good God! Why?"

"When you were talking, you looked almost cruelly pleased that you might have thought up a way of discovering who was selling the information."

"Stop imagining things."

She shook her head. It was not her imagination. There were times when his sharp hatred for criminals made it seem as if he were engaged on a personal crusade.

5

FUSIL had checked the morning's mail and reports and was about to leave for the mortuary when the internal telephone rang. The desk sergeant told him Kywood was on his way up. After replacing the receiver, Fusil swore.

Kywood was well built, sleek of features, with a strong chin that was an incorrect guide to his character. He was a man whose moods were conditioned almost wholly by the pressures on him, so that he would support his subordinates unless and until to continue to do so might jeopardise his own position. " 'Morning, Bob," he said, in a jovial voice.

Fusil answered, then added: "I'm just off to the P.M."

"That's all right, I shan't keep you a moment. I thought it better to come and have a word with you, though, instead of trying to talk over the 'phone. There's a bit of a problem cropped up."

Kywood pulled up a chair and sat down.

He offered a pack of cigarettes, though well aware that Fusil rarely smoked anything but a pipe, then lit one. "I had the chief constable on the telephone to me late last night, Bob. After he'd had dinner with Mr. Findren."

"Who?"

"Findren. The owner of the wine shop in the High Street — the place that used to supply the wines when George the Fifth stayed at Colnway Court. Findren had a moan."

"What about?"

"Surely you can imagine? You must know what's going on in your own department?"

"I usually have a good idea," said Fusil tightly.

"One of your men went into Findren's yesterday and asked them whether they'd bought any stolen whisky."

"What's so odd about that? I've had all pubs and bottle stores questioned."

"Can't you see that Findren was naturally upset that a detective should go into his store and ask such a question?"

"He shouldn't be so touchy."

Kywood looked angry, but his tone of voice remained pleasant. "Findren wouldn't buy stolen whisky. They're not that kind of place."

"You know as well as I do that in this sort of investigation all possible sources of information are questioned — whether or not they've served all the crowned heads of England since Magna Carta."

"Didn't you have a word with the Excise officer first?"

"Of course."

"What did he say?"

"He'd never met any irregularities at Findren, or anywhere else that I'm becoming interested in."

"Wasn't that good enough for you?" Kywood spoke earnestly. "Bob, I know it was only keenness made you do this, but you must learn that there are other considerations. The higher you rise in the force, the more you have to watch them. Did you realise that Findren is on the watch committee?"

"Is he?" said Fusil, with patent lack of interest.

Kywood's voice sharpened. "He's a very influential man on it, what's more — chairman of the finance sub-committee. Now I know in theory that sort of thing shouldn't make any real difference, but the hard facts of life are that it does, especially with a small borough force like ours."

"It's not going to stop me carrying out my duties as a policeman," said Fusil obstinately.

Kywood stood up and walked over to the window. He stared out at the depressing row of condemned Victorian houses. "You never take the trouble to be practical." He swung round. "Now just what was the point of going into a place like that and asking questions which were bound to upset people?"

"It was my duty . . . "

"It was your duty to use common-sense. As the chief constable said to me, what made you send a man in there to ask that sort of question when it's the one place in Fortrow you can guarantee is clean?"

"How can you guarantee that? Findren could have turned crooked."

"And the chief constable might have opened up a brothel," said Kywood heavily. "Bob," he continued, trying to sound like an uncle gently admonishing his favourite nephew, "in a small force like ours, duty and tact have to go hand-in-hand. If you want to get on, don't forget that."

Fusil said nothing. Kywood hesitated, then left.

Nothing so quickly angered Fusil as the intrusion of local politics into police work and this was one of the reasons why he was so in favour of the abolition of small, local forces. In Fortrow, council members seemed to think the police force was 'theirs', an employee to be rapped over the knuckles if it did anything they didn't like. The relationship between the public and any police force was a strange one — the public paid for and instructed the police to guard them, yet had to stand correction from them, and at all costs the police had to remain independent of the same public who paid their wages. Kywood would be better employed telling Findren that, he thought bitterly.

He left the police station and drove to the mortuary which was near the docks. The pathologist observed that Fusil was late and pointed out the obvious, that the post-mortem had started. Fusil apologised, though not with the best of grace, and he then crossed to the far wall and leaned against it, in company with the forensic scientist.

The pathologist worked quickly and deftly, all the time dictating notes to his secretary, and only paused when he wanted Detective Walsh to take a photograph. He had almost finished, when he spoke to Fusil. "I presume you would like finger-prints?"

"If that's possible, sir?"

"The fingers are badly burned on both hands, but the thumb and forefinger of the left hand were tucked under the body and haven't suffered quite such extensive damage. I may be able to get enough skin for prints from these two."

The pathologist used a small scalpel to strip off the burned skin from the print area of the thumb and forefinger and he carefully inserted these strips of skin into two tubes filled with formaldehyde solution. The tubes were labelled by the exhibits officer, who packed them in a special box and handed them on to Detective Sergeant Walsh.

The pathologist spoke pontifically. "You'll find, Sergeant, that the papillary ridges have been destroyed on the outer surface."

"Yes, sir," said Walsh. He disliked the pathologist, but managed to mask this fact.

"However, you'll be able to ascertain them from the inner surfaces."

"Yes, sir," said Walsh for the second time.

The pathologist handed the scalpel to his assistant and stripped off rubber apron and gloves. He crossed to the cracked wash-basin.

Fusil went up to him. "Can you give me a very quick run-down on anything you've discovered, sir?"

"You people are always in such a hurry." The pathologist filled the basin with warm water. He soaped his hands. "I found no cause of death other than by burning. The man was in his early twenties and in good physical condition except for a congenital abnormality in his right hip and a degenerated liver."

"What visible effect would the hip have had?"

"I'm just about to tell you," he snapped. "The abnormality wasn't sufficient to hinder him greatly and at its worst probably did no more than make certain movements of his right leg slightly unrhythmical. The liver was not yet sufficiently degenerated for him to have been aware of the condition. There were no signs of wounds, nor were any bones broken."

"If he didn't fall and break a leg, what stopped him escaping from the fire?" said Fusil, speaking more to himself than to the other. He stared at the body, now being sewn up by the assistant. How had the man come to die in the cellar?

The assistant at the county forensic laboratory examined the several pieces of charred wood which had been sent to Barstone from Fortrow. He carefully smelled them but could only catch the scent of charred wood. He chewed a piece of bread to clear his mouth, then wiped another piece of bread along the wood and chewed that, but again his only impression was one of charred wood.

From one of the wall cupboards, he took a widemouthed glass beaker, into which he put the pieces of charred wood. He covered the beaker, put it in a bowl of water, and heated the water until the thermometer recorded sixty-five degrees centigrade. He removed the beaker, opened it, and smelled the air inside. Faint, but quite unmistakable, was the oily smell of paraffin.

Kerr kicked back his chair in the general room and stood up. "This is driving me nuts."

Welland, working at his desk, looked up. "What's up with you, then?"

"D'you see that thundering great pile of shipping lists? The old man dumped them on me and told me to check through 'em and report back in half an hour's time."

"That's what I call being an optimist!" Welland grinned.

"I tell you what, Perry . . . " began Kerr.

"The answer is 'No'. I can't give you a hand."

"Have you forgotten that only the other day I spent hours and hours helping you?"

"And have you forgotten you only did that because the sarge ordered you to?" Welland sat back in his chair, which creaked. "I'll tell you something. Your Helen is a very brave little lady. If I were her, I wouldn't take you on."

"And if she was you, I wouldn't ask you," retorted Kerr.

Welland laughed boisterously.

"How about some coffee?" suggested Kerr.

"Sure. If you've got any."

"It's about your turn to find the tin."

"Where would I get that sort of money from?" He wagged a large finger at Kerr. "Don't you worry. Once you're married, your pockets won't know what the chink of silver is any more."

Kerr stared at him. "And you're the one who's always said how wonderful marriage is and I ought to get in on the act."

"Nothing like seeing someone else fall into the same trouble to ease one's pains." Welland again laughed boisterously.

Kerr boiled the electric kettle and made two cups of instant coffee. He and Welland each smoked with the coffee, then they returned to their work. Kerr once more struggled to list all the ships which had been in port for a period of fourteen days before and after each of the previous whisky robberies and for fourteen days prior to the present one. The D.I. had suggested it wasn't much of a job. The D.I. was dead wrong. Every ship in the world seemed to have been visiting Fortrow. He, Kerr, had once been told that a detective's work was ninety per cent hard slog and ten per cent detection: the proportions were wrong — they should have been ninety-nine and one.

He finished the task at half past twelve and when he checked each list against the others he discovered there was just one ship which had been in port on each occasion.

He lit another cigarette. It seemed that Fusil had known a thing or two after all — it must surely be more than a coincidence that this ship was always in port at the relevant time. He leaned back in the chair. There was something to be said for serving under a smooth, hard, sharp bastard like Fusil. For one thing, you learned the value of intelligent imagination.

When the cigarette was finished, he went through to Fusil's room but found it empty, so left a note to say what he had discovered. That done, he went down to the canteen, hoping Fusil would not return until he'd eaten.

Braddon liked life just the way it was. Other men might grow ulcers worrying about their promotion chances and fretting for success, but he just wanted things to continue as they were.

He stood at the long, scarred wooden counter of the Jack of Hearts and ordered another coffee. The café was no Ritz. The walls were dirty, the vinyl on the floor was worn out, the tables and chairs were badly battered from use, paper table-cloths were seldom provided, the ketchup bottles had thick rims of dried-up ketchup around their caps, and the menu was chalked up on a slate behind the counter. However, the prices were cheap, helpings large, and the food good. Open eighteen hours a day, there were seldom less than half the tables occupied.

Maddocks, the owner of the café, whose small, pinched face was badly scarred from childhood acne, brought him the coffee he'd ordered. Maddocks turned to leave, obviously eager to do so.

"Hang on," said Braddon.

Maddocks hesitated. Some of his

customers would not like to see him talking to a detective. "I'm busy," he muttered.

"You're not that busy," replied Braddon, good humouredly. He put three spoonfuls in the coffee.

"Look, Mister, one of your blokes 'as seen me. I told 'im all I knows."

"Perry's a nice lad, isn't he: Not been with us all that long." Braddon rubbed the tip of his nose. He often had a sleepy look about him, as if having difficulty in keeping his eyes open. "He's still a little bit too trusting."

Maddocks polished a glass with a wet and dirty cloth. A truck driver came up to the counter, shouted a ribald greeting, and ordered bangers, chips, and three eggs sunny-side up from the teen-age girl behind the counter who was usually ready to supplement her wages when off duty.

"Perry told me you said you'd heard nothing." Braddon looked at Maddocks over the top of the cup. "I reckon you'll have heard something interesting by now."

"I don't know nothing about that hi-jacking, Mister. You can search all you like and you won't find no nicked whisky round 'ere. Look, I've got work to do and it ain't good for trade, you being 'ere."

"D'you think people know I'm a detective?"

Maddocks looked quickly at Braddon to see if the detective was laughing: when he saw the glimmer of a smile in the other's bloodhound-like face, his expression became gloomy.

Braddon lit a cigarette. "If I was to get some news on this nicking, I likely wouldn't be back at all times of the day and night, disturbing trade."

Maddocks shrugged his shoulders in a gesture of tired defeat. "I don't know much," he said, in a whining voice.

"Let's hope it's enough."

Maddocks leaned forward and lowered his voice, although there was no one within earshot. "I 'eard a bloke was outside in 'is cab with a judy 'e'd picked up along the road — not in 'ere, mind. 'E saw 'em arrive in the van. Can't tell you no more than that."

"This bloke's name?"

"O'Farrell."

"Where does he live?"

"Can't rightly say, but 'e works for the millers in south Fortrow — that place by the central railway station. Drives their bulk tanker."

Braddon finished his coffee. "How much do I owe you?"

"Nothing."

"That's very civil of you. I must drop in again some time." He smiled when he saw the other's expression, which appealed to his simple sense of humour.

He drove back to Fortrow along the main road and then cut through a succession of side streets in order to avoid the centre of the town. The mill was very large, brick built, grimy with age, and it had a succession of descending roof lines which marked out the various additions that had been made over the years. There were two separate office buildings and a woman in the first of these gave him the information he wanted. O'Farrell lived in Bratby Cross. She checked a list and said he might still be around the mill because he was due to deliver a load of flour to one of the few remaining independent bakeries in the district.

He walked round the mill and found a

bulk tanker on the far side which had just taken on its load of flour. O'Farrell was about to climb up into the cab. Braddon introduced himself.

"What's up, then?" demanded O'Farrell, a little uneasily. He was a man of ordinary build, with the kind of grey anonymity that would hide him in any crowd.

"I'd like a word about Monday afternoon. You were in the park at the Jack of Hearts, weren't you?"

"So what if I was? I'm allowed to stop off for a cup of tea. The boss knows all about it."

"No one's getting at you for that. I'm only interested in what you saw of the whisky being hi-jacked?"

" 'Ere, 'ow did you know . . . ?"

"Does it matter?'said Braddon flatly.

"It's just . . . Look, I didn't see much."

"How come?"

"I weren't taking that much notice."

"Because of the woman you'd got with you?"

O'Farrell looked at him in obvious consternation.

"Married and worried the missus will get to hear?" diagnosed Braddon. "Not from me, she won't, not since you're going to help all you can."

O'Farrell licked his thin lips. "I wasn't . . . " He stopped.

"I don't suppose you were," said Braddon. He looked up at the cab of the tanker. "Be a bit tricky in there, wouldn't it?"

"Gawd!" exclaimed O'Farrell. Haltingly, he told Braddon what he had seen. The van had come in, gone right round, then come back through the first entrance and stopped by the lorry. Two men in mechanics' overalls had climbed out and gone to the lorry and he'd naturally assumed they were mechanics doing a job and because he was busy . . . that was to say . . . They'd just driven the truck out and the van had followed it.

"None of this seemed at all odd to you?" asked Braddon.

O'Farrell fidgeted with a screw valve on the tanker. "Mister, when a repair van comes along . . . "

"It obviously wasn't much of a repair they had to make if they were able to drive the lorry off almost immediately?"

"I didn't think like that."

He hadn't been in a fit state to think,

decided Braddon. "What did you notice about the men?"

"They were just men."

"Yeah, I know. But were they tall, short, fat, thin: Did you see their faces?"

"They were too far away for that. Anyway, they were wearing hats."

"Was there anything at all about them that you did notice? How did they walk? Did they talk to each other and could you hear their voices? How old were they?"

O'Farrell began to chew his lower lip. "One of 'em did walk a bit oddly, come to mention it."

"How d'you mean, oddly?"

"I don't rightly know."

Normally phlegmatic, Braddon suffered a desire to seize O'Farrell by the collar and shake him. "Are you saying he limped?"

"Not exactly limped, but it was as if one of 'is legs was stiff. Yeah, that's it. A stiff leg."

When Braddon left and returned to the car, his face accurately expressed his despondency. The lead had seemed so promising, yet now it had virtually petered out.

6

IN his office, Fusil sat back in his chair and closed his eyes. He must be getting old. Pressure of work was making him feel tired now where, five years before, it would not have done so.

If he was going to make the top ranks, he thought, eyes still shut, he'd have to get promotion before long. Of course, he wasn't going to hang on in the borough force, but if this became amalgamated in the county force in time, it would be difficult to know whether to remain then or to apply to another and larger force. A man could ruin his career by guessing wrongly at this stage: many a detective chief superintendent was less efficient, less able, than the detective inspectors under him, but had guessed right.

The telephone rang. The county forensic laboratory reported that traces of the drug, Pentothal, and some alcohol, had been found in the viscera of the dead man and traces of paraffin had been detected in the

90

charred wood. Fusil began to doodle on a sheet of paper. "What can you tell me about Pentothal?"

"It's an ultra-short action barbiturate, of anaesthetic duration. Alcohol adds dangerously to its hypnotic effect. If you've had an operation, you may have come across it. One moment you're conscious, the next you're not. It comes in powder form or solution. One interesting point, normally it's metabolised by the body and it's only if the liver is degenerated that you can expect to find traces of it. You'll remember, this man's liver was degenerated."

"He was drugged, then?"

"Depends in what sense you use the word. He could have been addicted to the stuff."

"To Pentothal?" asked Fusil, in surprise.

The scientist laughed harshly. "You can't name a barbiturate that someone hasn't become addicted to."

"Is there any way of proving he was addicted, or not?"

"We can't tell you. That information will have to come from your end."

Fusil dropped the pencil on to the

paper. "Even if he was addicted, surely he wouldn't take the stuff just before starting on a robbery?"

"Don't forget the alcohol. He could have taken a small dose that normally wouldn't have impaired his actions, then helped himself to a drink in the cellars — he might not have know^what hit him."

Fusil thought it unlikely that a villain addicted to Pentathol wouldn't know from experience the effects of adding alcohol, but he didn't argue. "Moving on to the traces of paraffin — can you say at what sort of concentration it was?"

"Not really, but the fact we could trace it that long after the fire means it was pretty generously applied."

After thanking the other, Fusil rang off. Assuming the manager of Verlay's was correct and was telling the truth, there had been no paraffin on the premises and therefore this fire had to be arson. Had the intruder, high on the barbiturate, poured himself out a quick drink after setting fire to the cellar and then collapsed? It made a very unlikely sequence of events.

Fusil left his room and went through to Braddon's. Braddon was talking on the telephone. As Fusil waited, he stared at the wall calendar which showed a young lady displaying as many of her natural charms as she was probably legally allowed to. In a vague sort of a way, he was surprised at Braddon's having such a calendar.

Braddon replaced the receiver. "That was the manager of the Northcote Company, sir. They can tell us the hydraulic jack was made five years ago, was probably sold in the south-east, and nothing more."

"Hell!" Fusil sat down on the edge of the desk. "Don't they believe in records?"

"Not the kind that will help us."

"Bloody inefficiency."

Braddon waited, then said: "I'm just back from the Jack of Hearts. The owner of the café gave me the name of a bloke who saw the villains arrive and nick the lorry."

"Did he!" exclaimed Fusil.

"It's no good, sir. I saw the bloke, O'Farrell. He was in the cab of his lorry with a broad. He was so het-up he hardly knew whether it was night or day."

"D'you mean to tell me he can't help at all?"

"He saw a van and two men. He doesn't

begin to know what the men looked like. He saw them drive the lorry off and never thought anything of it. About the only thing he did notice was that one of the men seemed to walk stiffly on one leg, but what . . . "

"Stiffly?" said Fusil sharply. "What's he mean — limping?"

"Not really limping — just not as smoothly as normal. But is that of any significance?"

"The P.M. found the dead man had a congenital hip defect which probably made him move with some slight difficulty."

Braddon thought about it and then shook his head. "But if the dead man helped nick the whisky, why bother to break into a wine shop that night? He'd have had enough booze to drown in."

"If it's the same man, the answer has to be that he didn't. He was murdered and the fire was to try and hide that fact."

"If it is the same man."

Fusil did not need to be reminded how tenuous was the evidence for this.

Below South Castle Gate, the only remaining medieval city gateway, the character of

High Street changed from a shopping area to one of commerce and the offices and warehouses became shabbier the nearer they were to the docks.

The shipping offices, half-way between South Castle Gate and the docks, were far more comfortable than the exterior of the building suggested. Kerr went in and came to the reception area which was staffed by an attractive brunette. He told her he'd come to see the marine superintendent. In the days before he'd been engaged, she'd have made a very tasty dish. She smiled at him and suggested he sit down while she telephoned Captain Elliott. As she spoke on the telephone, he noticed how slim was her waist. Just made for holding. Her smile had plainly said she was free for a night out.

Captain Elliott's office was up on the first floor. He was a youngish man, well dressed, and with a pleasant, friendly nature that was far removed from the traditional picture of an autocratic ship's captain.

"A considerable quantity of drink is loaded aboard the passenger ships for passenger consumption," said Captain

95

Elliott, in answer to Kerr. "This is especially so when they're off on a long trip to New Zealand and the west coast of U.S.A., or an extended cruise which starts from the U.S.A. But as to how many bottles of whisky go aboard and who knows when they're due, I just don't know. You need a word with someone who deals with catering. Would you like me to try to get hold of someone?"

"If you could, please."

Captain Elliott looked at his watch. "It's getting on, but Charlie should still be around. Charlie knows everything."

Charlie proved to be a middle-aged man in a rumpled suit, with horn-rimmed glasses and the harassed expression of someone who was underpaid yet was called on to cope with almost everything that went on in the office.

"Charlie," said Captain Elliott, "Detective Constable Kerr is from the local C.I.D. and he wants to know how all the whisky for the passengers is delivered to our ships, who's responsible for receiving it, who would know when it's due to arrive, and all that sort of thing."

Charlie had so hoarse and gravelly a

voice it was as if his vocal chords had been attacked with sandpaper. He had a habit of plucking at the lobe of his right ear. "At the end of each trip, the chief steward makes out his stores lists. They'll show the drink consumption over the past trip. Then, when he's told for certain the duration and destination of the next voyage, and how many passengers, he makes out a requisition note for all the drink he'll require."

"What happens to that?" asked Kerr.

"It comes to this office, is checked, and the orders are put through."

"Is the drink ordered direct from the distillers?"

"Depends on discounts and quantities. We usually get several tenders from various wholesalers and sometimes, when they deal direct, from distillers."

"Do you order direct from MacLaren?"

"We do, yeah. Just after they started the big advertising on the telly, they offered to deal direct with us for orders over a hundred cases at a time: they quoted delivery f.o.b. at a price a bob a bottle under anyone else. We've bought a lot of whisky from 'em, especially now it's got so popular. The wholesalers moaned, of course, but they couldn't match the price."

"Who would give the time of delivery?"

"This office. We say the time and dock and the distillers arrange it all. We've been let down, but it's never been MacLaren's fault — the stuff got pinched, like the other day. They've always got another load to us in time for sailing, though."

"Was the load you've just lost for the *Maltechara*?"

"That's right."

"And the whisky was for the same ship the other times?"

Charlie thought back. "That's odd! I'm pretty sure it was for her each time. Hey — what does that add up to?"

Kerr did not answer directly. "Who gives the distillers the actual delivery time?"

"Mostly, it's me," replied Charlie. "I like to see it aboard at least five days before she sails — that way, if there's any trouble there's time to put it right. Send a ship off without any Scotch aboard and you'll never hear the end of the complaints from the passengers."

"Would you tell someone aboard when

the whisky was due?"

"I give the chief steward the day and time."

"Who would he tell?"

"The stewards he'd need for the loading party. They have to load their own stores — always moaning about it. Never yet met a steward who liked work."

"Who's chief steward on the *Maltechara*?"

"Jackson. Been on her for several years, now. Come to think of it, he must be close to being the senior chief steward in the fleet."

"Would he be aboard?"

Charlie fiddled with the lobe of his ear. "Now you've got me," he admitted reluctantly.

"We can soon check," said Captain Elliott.

The chief steward was aboard the ship. Kerr thanked the two men for their help, then left the offices and caught a bus to the New Docks.

The New Docks — no complex of berths, but a two-mile long wharf — were in sharp contrast to the Old Docks. Built just before World War 2, almost bombed flat, and then rebuilt in the early 40s, they were clean, airy, and recently largely modernised, with special passenger terminals and bulk handling facilities. The M.V. *Maltechara* lay at berth 16. She was an eighteen-year-old, twenty-five-thousand-ton ship, modernised three years before at a sum greater than she had originally cost. In addition to her passenger accommodation there were four holds, three for'd and one aft, which carried chilled or frozen cargo homeward and general cargo outward.

Kerr boarded by the for'd of two gangways. A seaman asked him for his boarding pass and Kerr showed his warrant card. The seaman sullenly allowed him aboard.

Ships always offered romance to Kerr. They contained the mystery of foreign lands, the glamour of tropical islands, the beauty of moonlit seas. Even to walk down the long, featureless alleyways, off which were cross-alleyways and cabins, was to sample this romance . . . A night of calm with the ship barely moving to the gentle rolling Pacific swell. The moon, low in the tropical sky, sending its yellow-silver shaft across the sparkling water. The stars, as sharply bright as coruscating diamonds. Helen, nestling against him, loving, passionate, her horizons swept wide open by their tumultuous love . . . Hell, thought Kerr, where did one go to buy the tickets?

The chief steward's cabin was right down below, somewhere near the waterline, on B deck, just for'd of the complex of galleys, store rooms, and frozen food lockers.

The door to the cabin was open: Kerr knocked on it.

"Come on, come on, man. What's it now?" Jackson was working at his desk which was inches deep in papers.

"Mr. Jackson?"

Jackson looked round. "Yes?" He spoke testily. He was a large man, with a body that was rapidly slackening as muscle turned into fat. He was almost bald, his complexion was florid, and his cheeks bagged out as if he were squirrelling nuts inside them.

"Detective Constable Kerr, borough C.I.D."

Jackson's face was far too expressive: it portrayed first surprise, then fear.

Kerr stepped inside the cabin. "Would

you have a moment or two to answer some questions?"

"What . . . what's wrong?" Jackson muttered, trying to cover up his feelings and as a result beginning to speak far too quickly. "I mean, what brings the police aboard? It's the first time . . . It's years since . . . " He tailed off into silence, as if realising the contrary effect his hurried, scrambled words must have.

Kerr, unasked, sat down on the settee. One thing was certain — the chief steward was engaged in some sort of fiddle or he couldn't possibly be so upset by the arrival of one lowly D.C. "I'd like a word about the whisky that gets delivered aboard."

"The . . . the whisky?" croaked Jackson.

Kerr almost began to feel sorry for the other. "It's delivered each trip, isn't it, for the passenger stores?"

"That's right. But . . . "

"But what?"

"Nothing," mumbled Jackson.

"You know when a delivery of whisky is due?"

"No. That is . . . "

"Your shore office seemed to think you're always given the date and time of any coming delivery."

Jackson gulped heavily. "I . . . I didn't know that's what you were talking about," he said weakly.

"D'you pass this information on?"

"Of course not. Never."

"Then you don't have to detail any stewards who are going to load it?"

"Oh! . . . Oh, yes."

"How long beforehand do you tell them?"

Jackson began to sweat and he tried, absurdly, to wipe the sweat from his face under the guise of blowing his nose. "A . . . a couple of days."

"Have you ever told anyone else about the time and date of the deliveries of whisky?"

"Certainly not. Of course I haven't."

"Are you quite certain?"

The sweat rolled down Jackson's face.

"Has anyone ever approached you to try and discover when the whisky from MacLaren's distillery is due?"

"No."

"The facts suggest someone has."

"I swear it's not me."

"Four times a load of MacLaren whisky has been hijacked on the road. This is the only ship which has been in port on each occasion and the whisky was always for this ship."

"That doesn't prove anything." His voice rose. "I'm not the only person who knows about the deliveries. The people in the shore office know. Go and ask them . . ."

"We'll be questioning everyone who matters. We'll check bank accounts and savings accounts for unexplained sums of money. We'll be looking for regular housekeeping drawings that are suddenly stopped for a while — because money is being obtained from somewhere else. We'll search for a car that's too expensive for a bloke's wage, new furnishings in the house, too many visits to expensive restaurants . . . It's an odd fact how difficult it is to hide money if one tries to lead a normal, respectable life." Kerr sat back and waited. Fusil had taught him the value of silence.

He was watching Jackson closely and he saw a sudden tightening of the other's mouth. That could surely signify only one thing — Jackson, frightened and frantic, was desperately going to try and save himself by denying everything, no matter what the evidence against him might be.

Kerr spoke in a casual, almost bored voice, as if he didn't give a damn what the other did. "With a first offender, the courts are often lenient — provided that first offender has helped the police in their investigations. Of course, if he's tried to obstruct them, the courts play it really rough." The judges' rules, thought Kerr, would not approve of what he'd said — they'd term his words both threat and inducement: but something else Fusil had taught him was that in times of mental stress few 'amateurs' would ever remember the exact words a detective used.

Jackson's features dissolved into an expression of acute misery. He tried to speak twice, but couldn't find the words. He looked at Kerr, then away. He licked his lips. "I . . . I didn't realise . . . I mean I thought it wouldn't really matter . . . "

No one could deny the brilliance of his interrogation, thought Kerr.

"So you persuaded him to confess," said Fusil. He looked up. "What are you waiting for now? Immediate promotion?"

"No, sir," said Kerr stiffly.

"That's just as well, isn't it?" Fusil

smiled. "Did you take a statement and get him to sign it?"

"Yes, sir, here it is." Kerr handed over his notebook.

Fusil read through the statement. "Blast!" he muttered. "Doesn't get us very far, does it? Still, that's not your fault," he added, with rare magnanimity. "Well done. Leave the notebook with me."

Looking pleased with himself, Kerr went out.

Fusil began to read the statement through again, but was interrupted by the telephone. It was a call from county H.Q. The finger-prints of the dead man had been identified as being Edward Finnigan's. He had plenty of form.

After writing down Finnigan's last known address, Fusil rang off. He began to tap on the desk with his fingers. Had Finnigan and others conceived the whisky job and carried it out from the beginning, or had they merely been employed to do the hi-jacking? The answer to this would tell whether there was a centre-man. How in the hell was the whisky being disposed of?

7

FUSIL stared down at the list of all the wine shops and wholesalers in Fortrow. Out of all the names there, only two had a sufficient trade in MacLaren whisky to be able to absorb the quantities which had been stolen over the past two years.

Who'd organised the thefts? A Londoner? Wouldn't a London villain have employed a London mob to carry out the hi-jacking? Yet Finnigan was a local villain. Again, Finnigan had been murdered — why? — several hours after the hi-jacking. Surely it was inconceivable that any London mob would have hung around Fortrow that long? Accept the theft had been organised locally and the stolen whisky was being flogged locally, how was the sale of it being covered up? A few bottles to each pub? There weren't nearly enough pubs in the area and not a single publican reported any such approach. Were the labels on the export bottles being soaked off and being replaced by ordinary labels? All the labels from the bottles which his D.C.s had brought in had been rushed up to MacLaren by passenger train, car, and aircraft for expert examination. The result: All had been declared genuine. (The police canteen supervisor had moaned like hell at having to buy so many unlabelled bottles of MacLaren whisky all at the same time.) Then how were the bottles being sold, if they were being sold locally? This question brought him back in a full circle to Findren and Sharman. Only they had the volume of sales to provide the necessary cover.

The more he thought about it, the more certain he was that it was a local job from beginning to end. So? So he must question Sharman and Findren — remembering Kerr's assessment of Sharman and, perhaps, Kywood's comments regarding Findren.

Fusil parked his car outside Sharman's warehouse and he and Kerr went into the office. Mrs. Sharman was working in the reception area. She recognised Kerr. "Still in trouble?"

"Still in trouble," he answered. She was as immaculately turned out as before, with make-up that suited her to a T, not a hair on her head out of place, and a dress that hugged her body even more closely than had the previous one. She wore a beautiful pearl necklace that would have been worth a small fortune if real. Perhaps the only hint of a fault was the suggestion of a certain toughness of character — yet wasn't it a well-known fact that toughness in a woman could turn into flaming, lyrical passion if the right man . . . Kerr sighed.

"Can I help you," she asked, "or is it my husband you want to see?"

"We'd like a word with Mr. Sharman, please," said Fusil.

She stared at him for a moment, her face almost expressionless, then she said: "Can I give him your name?"

"Detective Inspector Fusil."

"I shan't be long." She left.

Kerr went to speak, but Fusil turned away and began to pace the floor. Mrs. Sharman returned in under the half minute. "He's in the warehouse. You know the way, don't you?" she said to Kerr.

"I always know the way to the nearest drink," replied Kerr cheerfully. She smiled at him as he followed Fusil out. Quite definitely, he thought, she was one very hot potato.

Sharman was loading wooden cases on to one of two electrically driven fork-trucks and was sweating freely. "Still got your problems, the wife says, and some of the big brass come along? Still — gives me a chance for a break." He sat down on a wooden case. "I've been humping bottles since eight-thirty this morning and they're beginning to become very heavy."

"Not got any help then?" asked Fusil.

"I employ one bloke, who drives the van around on deliveries to the shops as well as giving a hand in here. We started small, Inspector, and here at the warehouse we've remained small. That's the secret of success today. If you employ too many people, you find you're paying a full week's wage for half a week's work." He laughed. "Private business isn't like one financed by the rates — got to make it pay, we have."

"We reckon to earn our salaries," said Fusil tightly, quickly angered by the other's tone of voice and words. He looked round the warehouse. "You've a fair-sized stock."

"Something over thirty thousand quid's worth."

Kerr whistled.

"I'll tell you both something. When we started business, the wife and me, we didn't know the meaning of a thousand quid. Now I've got so that it doesn't mean anything more than a fiver did at the beginning." He brought his cigar case from his pocket, pointed to a large notice which said 'No Smoking', winked, and proffered the case. Fusil refused, Kerr accepted.

"Ours is a funny business, you know," Sharman continued. "Teaches you something about human psychology, just like yours must do?" He looked across at Fusil, but received no acknowledgement of his words. "I could knock another bob off some bottles, but don't. That would be too much. The public, bless 'em, likes a good bargain but gets mighty suspicious of a very good one. The man or woman says: 'How can they sell a bottle of gin for all that much less than the other bloke? I'll lay they water it down.' So we keep just below everyone else, make a bit more profit because the public's suspicious, and everybody's happy." He chuckled loudly, then lit his cigar. "S P Q R, as my dad always said."

"S P Q R?" queried Fusil.

"Small profits, quick returns."

Fusil showed his annoyance at having asked so obvious a question.

"We started with one shop," said Sharman, with relish, "tucked away out of sight in Portman Street. Everyone said we were proper daft. Now we've four shops in this town, three in others, and we're due to open an eighth pretty soon. Trade's increasing so fast I'm running out of graph paper!" He laughed again.

"Very interesting," said Fusil. "Do you sell much MacLaren whisky?"

"Aye, we do that, mon," replied Sharman, in a travesty of a Scottish accent.

Kerr looked at Fusil and was not surprised to see the expression of dislike on the D.I.'s face.

"How much do you sell a month?" asked Fusil.

"I wouldna ken precisely, mon." He suddenly reverted to his normal voice, which had a faint trace of a Cockney accent. "I'd guess around three thousand, except at Christmas time when it's a lot more before and a lot less after." He jabbed the air with his cigar. "That pile over there is MacLaren whisky. That'll tell you how popular it is."

Fusil and Kerr looked across the warehouse. At the far end was a pile of cardboard cases which had been stacked in a rough rectangle, four feet high.

"The public really goes for MacLaren these days," said Sharman, "which only goes to show what publicity can do. You know the slogan — 'every man a connoisseur'. What a thought!" He laughed scornfully. "Still, it suits us as we deal direct with the distillery and thereby get a better discount."

"How many bottles have you in store now?" demanded Fusil.

"I'll have to check up on that." Sharman wriggled his way off the trailer and walked across to a small glassed-in office area which was to the right of the warehouse doors. He went in and they saw him looking through some books and making notes on a pad. He returned a few minutes later. "As of this morning, one thousand nine hundred and forty-three bottles. And if I'm more than a hundred out, they'll sack me." He laughed again, with a boisterous self-satisfaction.

"Have you any objection to my looking at your books?" asked Fusil.

"Objection? None whatsoever, old man. Still trying to trace the stolen whisky? You can search my figures until the moon turns blue and you won't find any and that's straight." He chuckled. "Not that I wouldn't mind a few — they'd offer an O P Q R and no mistake."

Fusil made a point of not asking what these initials stood for.

Kerr watched Fusil and Sharman go into the glass-enclosed office. Sharman opened up some books and began to talk. Kerr couldn't hear what was being said, but from Fusil's expression and from the way Sharman was laughing more and more broadly, things weren't going as Fusil liked them to.

Fusil led the way back into the warehouse. "I want to check the numbers," he said belligerently.

"You do whatever you like, Inspector. Count everything ten times over and divide by the number you first thought of!" Sharman winked at Kerr, an action that did not go unremarked by Fusil.

"Come on," snapped Fusil at Kerr,

and he marched across the centre of the warehouse rather as if about to engage in battle. He crossed to some metal racks and pulled out bottles from them, looking briefly at the labels before pushing them back in.

"Those are the ones I paid two bob cash for," said Sharman. "A three-legged man sold 'em to me."

Fusil's expression darkened. "Kerr," he snapped, "don't just stand there. Get on and count."

Kerr began to count bottles of whisky of brands other than MacLaren. Before long, he'd made a mistake and had to go back to the beginning. Fusil spoke sarcastically and Sharman began the childish trick of counting aloud to confuse. Kerr took out his notebook and jotted down the numbers in tens. When he came to the bottles of MacLaren whisky in the racks, he counted them twice to make certain he got the number right.

Fusil went over to the pile of cardboard cases of MacLaren whisky. He picked up one, turned, and stumbled slightly.

Sharman spoke loudly. "Like a hand, Inspector maybe it's too heavy for you?"

Kerr grinned and then hastily assumed a blank expression when he saw the D.I. was glaring at him.

Fusil put the case down on the concrete floor. "I'd like to open this."

"Sure. Use this knife." Sharman took a penknife from his overalls and offered it.

Fusil used the knife to slit through the brown paper taping to free the lid of the box. He pulled out a bottle of whisky and examined the label. It was not an export one. He dropped the bottle back into its compartment.

"Would you like to keep that as a memento of your visit, Inspector?" asked Sharman.

"No," said Fusil.

"Go on, be a devil! No one's watching you."

Fusil seemed to be about to speak, but at the last moment he managed to control himself.

Sharman stepped forward to the opened case and pulled out a bottle. He spoke to Kerr with undiminished good humour. "What about you, then? You don't look T.T. to me. Drink this on the firm." He lobbed the bottle across to Kerr, who caught it and then suffered some difficulty in knowing what to do with it.

"Have you counted these boxes?" demanded Fusil, in a voice thick with rage.

"No, sir," replied Kerr. "I was just . . . "

"Goddamn it, can't you do anything without being told?"

Kerr put down the bottle and began to count the boxes. Fusil moved round the warehouse, pulling bottles out of racks at random and frequently demanding to open up other cases in other piles — requests which Sharman met without a second's hesitation. Fusil found no more MacLaren whisky. Satisfied there was nothing more he could do, he stalked over to the doors and called Kerr across.

"Have you finished?" asked Sharman.

"Yes," snapped Fusil.

"I don't think you had a look at those bottles over there . . . "

"Thank you for your help," muttered Fusil, as if the words hurt to speak. He left.

As Kerr came alongside Sharman, Sharman said: "Don't ever give him vinegar to drink — might turn the vinegar sour!"

He roared with laughter.

When in a bad temper, Fusil's driving became even worse than usual. He backed into a stanchion without doing too much damage. Then, when they were driving out from the estate on to the ordinary road, he came out slap in front of a lorry which had to brake very sharply. The lorry driver leaned out of his cab and shouted obscenities. Fusil threatened to arrest him.

Kerr was just beginning to relax when Fusil said: "Well?"

"Well what, sir?"

"What the hell did you mean by accepting that bottle of whisky?"

Kerr looked down at the bottle in his lap. "It was just that he seemed to want to give it to one of us, sir. I didn't like to offend him."

"You know the rules."

"Surely one bottle . . . "

"It's the principle, not the quantity, as you ought to know."

"Yes, sir."

There was a silence. Fusil drove past a wobbling cyclist and somehow managed to miss him. "How many bottles of whisky were there?" he snapped.

Kerr took his notebook from his pocket. "I made it four hundred and forty bottles in the racks and a hundred and twenty-five cases."

"I'm not a travelling computer. How many bottles in the cases?"

Kerr worked it out. "Fifteen hundred, sir. So it's nineteen hundred and forty all told."

"Have you taken off the one you pinched?"

"I . . . No, sir."

Fusil braked and then blew the horn at the car in front. "The figures agree," he muttered.

Welland hardly ever worried about promotion: the future seldom concerned him. Life was good, life was for enjoying, and the future could look after itself. Ironically, this carefree attitude to the world and his work had allowed him to build up a better chain of informers than if he had been a man more seriously dedicated to his work: the informers seemed to trust him more for being unambitious.

He met Fitch in Durall Park. Fitch was

tall and thin and he had a long scar on his cheek which came from the time he'd been chivved in prison with a sharpened watch spring.

Welland passed over a pack of cigarettes and then sat back on the painted wooden seat in the warm sunshine. "We're interested in whisky," he said.

"The load what was nicked on Monday?" Fitch's eyes were never still: he was always looking round, checking on everyone in sight. "Ain't 'eard a whisper."

"The whisky must be on offer?"

"I'm tellin' you straight, Mister, I ain't 'eard nothing."

Welland lit a cigarette. "D'you know Finnigan?"

"Ed Finnigan? Yeah."

"Have you seen him around recently with anyone?"

"I could've."

Welland passed across two one-pound notes.

" 'E's been with Ginger Playford and Abe Stretley."

"Who are they?"

"Ginger's a tearaway. Abe's got brains."

"When did you last see them together?"

"Can't rightly remember."

Welland produced his wallet and pulled out of it a one-pound note. "That's got me real skint." He passed the note across.

"It were Monday. They was all in a boozer at lunchtime."

"Which boozer?"

"The Jolly Admiral, down by the docks."

"Have you any idea when they left there?"

"Don't know nothing more than that, Mister." Fitch suddenly stood up and hurried away.

Welland vaguely wondered if something had alarmed the other, then sat back to enjoy the sunshine. Who could complain that coppering wasn't a good job?

Pills, the manager, escorted Fusil and Kerr along the dark passage and to the door marked 'Chairman', on which he knocked. He opened the door and stepped inside. "The police, sir," he said, in deferential tones. He waited until the detectives were inside, then left.

Shades of the nineteen hundreds, thought Kerr. The room was gloomy because the windows were small and the dark wooden panelling absorbed much of what light did enter. On the walls hung a number of paintings of men, most of whom looked smugly self-satisfied. A framed royal warrant was above the heavy marble fireplace. The desk was made of ancient mahogany and it could easily have accommodated not only the chairman of the firm, but also his board of directors.

Findren was a small turkey-cock of a man, with bristling white moustache, a regimental tie, and a country check suit. His tone of voice was antagonistic, as if perpetually ready to have an argument. "I fail utterly to understand the purpose of your visit," he said, not bothering with any form of greeting.

"We're checking on the load of . . . " began Fusil.

"I'm well aware of the work in which you're engaged. What I said was, I fail to understand the purpose of your visit here."

Kerr stared at him with a dislike that was immediate and automatic. Did the little bastard think he was colonel-in-chief, addressing the licentious soldiery?

Findren's voice became still more

challenging. "Are you accusing either myself or my firm of engaging in the trade of stolen whisky?"

"I'm accusing no one of anything, sir."

"Then will you please explain why you're here?"

"Our job calls on us to establish the innocence of some people, however certain we may think them innocent, just as we have to prove the guilt of others, however certain we may be of their guilt."

"You distinguish between establish and prove. Are you here to establish or to prove?"

"I'm here to do my duty, sir."

Findren brushed his forefinger along the right-hand side of his moustache, then the left-hand. "Enquiries have already been made here by your staff."

"Quite so, sir."

"Then either the previous enquiry was incompetently handled or your presence here today is an impertinence and you are deliberately casting a slur on the name of my firm."

"I'm casting no slur."

"Inspector, at least do me the honour of not treating me as a fool. You would not come here unless you thought your visit necessary, and you would not consider your visit necessary unless you mistakenly believed my firm could be engaged in trading in stolen whisky."

There was a pause.

Findren again brushed his moustache with crooked finger. "You are presumably not unaware of the position I hold on the watch committee?"

Fusil's temper momentarily overflowed. "There's only one position of authority in this country which lifts a person above a police investigation and that's the reigning monarch."

Findren flushed. "I do not need you to teach me constitutional history," he snapped.

There was another and longer pause.

"What do you want here?" demanded Findren curtly.

"I wish to examine your stocks of wine and whisky, sir," said Fusil.

"My staff has previously made it abundantly clear that there is no point to any such examination."

"I'd still like to make it."

"Inspector," said Findren, "I shall make

a very full report of your attitude."

"That is your privilege."

"I shall not overlook your insolence."

"My detective constable will bear witness that I have said nothing insulting."

Findren looked contemptuously at Kerr. He stomped over to his chair behind his desk, sat down, picked up the nearer telephone and spoke to his manager. "Take the policemen down to the cellars. See they don't pinch anything," he added.

Anger whitened Fusil's face, but he managed to say nothing.

The manager escorted them down to three interconnected cellars. His manner was nervously friendly, as if trying to tell them that he didn't really suspect their intentions, but he did have to watch because his boss had ordered it.

The whisky, along with all other spirits, was in the third cellar, in metal racks. An easily conducted count showed there to be five hundred and twelve bottles of MacLaren whisky. Fusil picked out a number of the bottles, but none bore export labels. He went round the racks, checking on the other bottles of spirits and ordered Kerr into the next cellar.

Kerr walked under the low archway with bent shoulders and then straightened up. The place looked to be under six inches of dust and cobwebs — didn't anyone ever clean up? He picked up a bottle from one of the racks and tried to brush the dust off the label to see what it contained.

"Oh, my God!" cried the manager, who had just followed him, "put that down."

The voice startled Kerr and he let go of the bottle, catching it again just in time. He held it upside down by its neck. "No need to panic," he said cheerfully, "it's still in one piece."

The manager began to stutter. "That . . . that's a bot . . . bottle of Château Latour twenty-nine. Please, please, don't shake it."

"What's so special about it?"

The manager came forward and took the bottle from Kerr. He slowly lowered it to a horizontal position and then replaced it in the rack as if it were egg-shell thin. "If Mr. Findren ever learns . . ." He shook his head, his expression almost frightened. "Those two dozen are for Lord Tasketh. There aren't another couple of dozen of twenty-nines this side of London. They're worth ten pounds a bottle, or more."

"How much?" said Kerr, in tones of incredulity. "For a drop of old vino? Some people have more money than sense, that's for sure."

"You don't understand," said the manager plaintively. "You ... you haven't moved anything else?"

"Not yet."

"Please don't touch any other bottles in this bin. What could I have said to Mr. Findren if you'd dropped that one? What could I have said?"

"You could have told the old faggot he was ten quid the poorer," replied Kerr, cheerfully forgetting the need for diplomacy.

8

KERR was about to leave the general room that evening, with the bottle of whisky that Sharman had given him, when Fusil walked in.

The D.I. looked round the room. "Why the hell can't you ever keep this place tidy?" he demanded.

Reluctantly, Kerr had to agree that it was a little untidy. In one corner were a number of obscene books and photographic magazines, remarkable for their complete lack of originality, found in an abandoned stolen car, in another corner were the two pairs of overalls they had worn while examining the debris in the burned-out wine store, and on the floor by Rowan's desk was a large heap of brown paper that had been ripped off the parcels taken from a small-time sneak-thief.

"Get this cleaned up by tomorrow," ordered Fusil. "In the meantime, come along with me."

"But I'm just off, sir."

"You're dead right, there. You're just off with me to go and interview a likely villain." Fusil turned and left the room.

The D.I.'s temper was inclined to be sharp at the best of times, thought Kerr, but after their interviews with Findren and Sharman it had become explosive. Why was it . . .

"Kerr," came a distant shout, remarkable for its quality of anger.

He hurried out of the room and down to the courtyard and the D.I.'s car.

Fusil drove out on to the road with a rush. A pedestrian saved himself by hastily stepping back. "Bloody fool," muttered Fusil.

Kerr leaned back in the seat and tried to concentrate on the problem of whether there was any chance he could get word to Helen that he would be late.

"We're going to see Playford," said Fusil abruptly. "I've sent Braddon and Rowan to question Stretley."

"Who's Playford, sir?"

"Don't you ever bother to know what's going on?" demanded Fusil, turning to glare at Kerr. When he looked back at the road, they were heading straight for a parked car. He wrenched the wheel over.

Would they ever get to Playford? wondered Kerr.

"Playford and Stretley were with Finnigan in a dockside pub on Monday at lunchtime." Fusil's tone of voice was calmer. "The two of them have got more form than Finnigan had. It's a hundred to one they're our mark."

"Have we any proof that they and Finnigan carried out the hi-jacking? Have we even any real proof, sir, that Finnigan was one of the hi-jackers?"

"No."

"Then why . . . " Kerr stopped.

"Why are we moving so obviously? Because all our leads are drying up. Questioning Jackson again hasn't added anything, we're not getting anywhere fast, and the case is going stale. So I've secured a search warrant — we may turn up something." Fusil spoke scornfully. "The old fool of a magistrate tried not to issue it to me: said there wasn't really enough evidence. I had to improvise."

It was typical of Fusil to bend the evidence to get the search warrant, thought Kerr. The moment the D.I. became impatient, he began taking risks. Was it really worth doing this? Weren't there more senior officers in any force who'd never taken any real risks than there were those who had?

"We've only one joker to play," went on Fusil. "We've made a point of not publishing the name of the dead man. If they didn't murder Finnigan, they'll not yet know what happened to him."

Hardly a very effective joker, thought Kerr. These days, real villains knew their law: they knew it well enough to use it.

They entered an area of mean and depressing streets. Terraces of houses were all similar in size and construction and the front gardens were too small to be anything but patches of drabness.

Fusil spoke suddenly. "I have a recurring nightmare. Whenever I pass through this part of town, I imagine myself condemned by fate to live in it. I can feel the greyness closing in and choking me."

Kerr was astonished on two scores: that Fusil should ever believe he could fail in life sufficiently to be condemned to live in such an area and that he should ever admit to this. Kerr looked very quickly sideways at the D.I. It was odd how very little you really knew about people, he thought. For most of the time, Fusil appeared to be just a razor-sharp, self-sufficient, supremely confident D.I. who believed there were twenty-five hours in every day ... Yet very occasionally he offered a momentary glimpse of himself worrying, fearing, harried by the kind of doubts that any ordinary man knew. Hadn't Shakespeare put it very clearly in one of his interminable plays? Or was he mixing up the reference with the very true saying that all cats were the same in the dark?

Someone had tried to make something of the pocket-sized front garden of Number 59, Arcoll Avenue. Five hybrid tea-roses had been planted in the bed. Unfortunately, the roses seemed to have been washed by the greyness of the area and their colours looked faded. The front door had been newly painted, but the light fawn showed streaks of dirt.

Mrs. Playford answered Fusil's knock. She was a small, bird-like woman, with an air of harassment, as if life were one long rush. When Fusil introduced himself, she instinctively put her hand to her mouth in a gesture of fright.

"May we come in?" he asked. There was sympathy in his voice.

Wordlessly, she opened the door wider and they stepped inside. The hall was spotlessly clean and smelled of polish. Some Middle Eastern copper coffee pots with long curving spouts stood on the window shelf and glinted in the light.

"Is Ginger in?" asked Fusil.

"I . . . I don't know," she answered, obviously lying.

"I'd like a word with him, Mrs. Playford."

She hesitated, trying to find the courage to refuse, but eventually failing. She showed them into the front room and then mumbled that she'd try to find him. After she'd gone, Fusil crossed to the mantelpiece and looked at the group of family photographs. One of these was of Mrs. Playford and her three sons. Two of the sons, he knew, were hardworking and honest: Ginger Playford was a villain. What had led one member of this very ordinary family into villaining?

When Ginger Playford came into the room, his attitude was one of hostile insolence. "Well — what's to do then?"

Mrs. Playford stood in the doorway. She looked at her son, at Fusil, then back at her son again. Her expression became one of bitter, defeated despair. She seemed about to speak, but left without saying a word.

Playford stood by an arm-chair and lit a cigarette. "Speak up, mate. I ain't got all day to waste."

"Have you been busy lately?" asked Fusil.

"I'm always busy." Playford swung round and spoke to Kerr. "You shove that down in your little notebook."

"Been out on some jobs?" asked Fusil.

"I've been working legal, down at the docks. So don't you come shading me."

Fusil smiled sarcastically.

Playford, wearing a T-shirt and jeans, scratched the back of his neck. "Do me a favour. Say what you've got to say and then 'op it."

"When did you do your last job?"

"I ain't done one since the time you bastards nicked me."

"So you haven't been doing any driving lately?"

Playford's manner changed: he became a shade less belligerent. "I've got me own car, if that's what you mean."

"Someone told me you've been driving a van around the place?"

"It's a lie."

"Then you weren't out in one on Monday afternoon?"

Playford became very interested in the cigarette he was smoking.

"Would you have called in at the Jack of Hearts for a cuppa?"

"No."

"D'you know the café?"

" 'Course."

"When were you last there?"

"Can't remember." He crossed to the settee and flopped down on it. He flicked the ash from his cigarette on to the carpet.

"Someone seems to think you were there in a van." Fusil began to fill the bowl of his pipe with tobacco, shredding the tobacco with slow and deliberate movements. He looked up. "Who were you with?"

"I told you, I wasn't there." Playford threw the cigarette, only half smoked, into the fireplace.

"Abe Stretley?"

Playford lit another cigarette.

"D'you know Abe?" asked Fusil.

"Not really."

"How about Ed Finnigan?"

"No." Playford turned his head so that neither detective could clearly see his face.

"You weren't with either of them on Monday afternoon?" asked Fusil, in the same even voice.

"No," shouted Playford.

"I wonder why you're lying?"

"I ain't."

"Didn't you have a jar with Ed and Abe at The Jolly Admiral on Monday?"

Playford drew on the cigarette. "All right," he muttered. "So me and them 'ad a drink together."

"And it was this Monday?"

"It could've been."

"That's fine. Now I wonder why you bothered to lie about knowing them?"

"I wouldn't tell a split the bleeding time of day."

Fusil struck a match and lit his pipe. "I'd say you'd only deny knowing them if there was a very good reason for doing so. Maybe you all did a job together?" He dropped the spent match into an ash-tray. "I wonder if the three of you hi-jacked that whisky lorry?"

"No."

"And then you and Abe murdered Ed?"

Playford swung round. "We done what?" he cried.

"Murdered Ed. Burned him to death in the wine shop."

There was no doubting the fact that Playford was shocked. "You . . . you're trying it on?"

"We identified his body this morning," lied Fusil. "I've come to pick you up for his murder."

"We ain't murdered 'im. When we left 'im be'ind . . . " Playford stopped suddenly.

"When you left him behind?" said Fusil softly.

Playford threw his cigarette into the fireplace. He immediately lit another.

"We've got you for a lifer," said Fusil. "Unless it was Abe did the killing? If that's the way it was, you'd better start talking quick."

The two detectives watched Playford's face. They saw indecision and then defiance: they knew the interview had just failed.

"We 'ad a drink at the pub and split up after. I don't know nothing more," muttered Playford.

Fusil stood up and took a folded sheet of paper from his inside pocket. "Here's a search warrant. We'll start off by seeing what you've got on you."

Playford jumped to his feet.

"Search him," ordered Fusil.

Kerr approached Playford and stood in front of him. Kerr, having put the notebook in his coat pocket, held his fists clenched, his right knee ready, and his weight on his left leg.

Playford relaxed. Kerr searched him and found nothing.

They went upstairs, watched from the end of the hall by Mrs. Playford, to Playford's bedroom. It was newly decorated and neat and tidy. They searched the chest-of-drawers, the wardrobe and all the clothes hanging in it, and the bed. In a small slit in the mattress, they found two hundred and sixty-three pounds in one-pound notes.

Fusil examined the notes.

"I won that on the dogs," said Playford.

"Let's have something more original

than that," replied Fusil, in a bored voice.

"I'm telling you, I won it on the dogs."

"What's the name of the bookie and which track was it at?"

"Several tracks, up in the Smoke."

"The names of the bookies?"

"Can't remember."

"What dates?"

"I go regular. Can't say exactly what dates."

"Which dogs won?"

"I can't remember. I just keep backing."

Fusil stared at the thick bundle of money in his hand. Playford's explanation for the money was a hoary old chestnut, but it was one very difficult to disprove.

"Give us the money," demanded Playford.

Fusil swore silently. Without the necessary provable evidence, he was going to have to hand it back.

Braddon reported to Fusil, back at the station. "No luck, sir," he said, more lugubriously than ever. "Stretley eventually admitted drinking with Finnigan and Playford, but says they split up as soon as they left the pub."

"How did he take the news of Finnigan?"

"He was shocked, but he didn't change his story."

"Did you find anything in the house?"

"Nothing useful."

9

WHEN Kerr, parcel in hand, arrived at Helen's house that night, she said: "You're only three hours late this time, so I suppose I shouldn't complain."

"I'm most terribly sorry, darling, but . . . "

"But you were held up and just couldn't get to a 'phone — honest." She linked her arm with his.

"As a matter of fact, it wasn't quite like that. I've a confession to make."

"Oh?" She began to frown slightly.

"I was just leaving the station when a blue Ferrari drew up. There was a gorgeous bit of crackling driving it and she leaned across and said she was lonely and would I . . . "

"John Kerr," said Helen forcefully, "there are times when your so-called sense of humour positively stinks."

They went into the sitting-room. He apologised to Mrs. Barley for being late and she said it didn't matter a bit as she hadn't planned an early meal.

Kerr handed the parcel to Mr. Barley. "We had to visit a booze place today and they handed out a sample. Thought you might like it."

Mr. Barley unwrapped the bottle. "That's real nice of you, John, but are you sure you don't want it . . . ?" His question was asked for form only, as they all knew. He loved whisky but, now that he was retired, was seldom able to afford it.

"I don't know whether you like MacLaren malt?" said Kerr, as he sat down on the settee.

"There's nothing as good as a drop of real malt whisky, John." Mr. Barley turned and spoke to his wife. "Remember the stuff we had when we went up to the Highlands?"

"I remember you drank far too much and tried to do a Scottish Reel and twisted your back."

He grinned, in an embarrassed way. "It was a lovely drop of malt whisky. Never tasted anything like it since."

"And that's a very good job!" said Mrs. Barley. "Well, I'll get the supper."

"No hurry, Ducks. Let's have a little drink first. A bit of a celebration, like."

He took off his spectacles and polished them with a handkerchief. "We haven't really drunk to Helen and John yet."

"I suppose the stew won't come to any harm for a while longer." She settled back in her chair.

There was a strange exhilaration to genuine happiness, thought Kerr, a glow that explained why life was so precious a gift. It was one of the many discoveries he had made since meeting Helen.

Fusil and Josephine were watching television when the front door-bell rang. "Who in the world can that be at this time of night?" she said.

"I'll find out and send 'em packing." He stood up, yawned, and stretched.

The door-bell rang again.

"You can tell 'em we're not deaf," she said.

When he opened the front door, he found the caller was Kywood. "By God, Bob, there's trouble!" Kywood, uninvited, stepped into the hall. "I've just had a bellyful from the chief constable. He's been on the 'phone for over a quarter of an hour . . . "

Fusil opened the dining-room door. "Shall we go in here, sir?"

Kywood walked forward. "I don't mind telling you, he was in a state. He started off by . . . "

"I'll be with you in a minute," interrupted Fusil. He returned to the sitting-room. "It's the D.C.I., in a panic."

"Really, Bob, this is the limit," snapped Josephine. "You didn't get home until after nine o'clock and now he dares to come bursting in here just as you're relaxing." Her indignation was bitter. She was always worrying because Fusil worked so hard.

"Can you rustle up some coffee?"

"No, I damn' well can't," she answered, even as she stood up. She fought some of his battles harder than he fought them himself. In consequence, some people were convinced she was a prize bitch — yet intrinsically there was nothing hard about her.

He grinned. "Put a good pinch of arsenic in one of the cups, if you like — but remember which one it's in."

He went back to the sitting-room.

"Bob, what's going on?" demanded Kywood. "The chief constable says

Findren's complained you went and questioned him earlier today. But you can't have done, not after what I said to you . . . "

"I questioned him at his office, yes, sir."

Kywood rubbed his hand across his forehead. "But didn't you understand a word of what I said to you the other day?"

"Of course. But I've a murder and a hi-jacking to clear up."

"You didn't . . . " Kywood lowered his voice. "You . . . didn't accuse him of being the murderer?"

"No."

"Thank God for that!" Kywood took a handkerchief from his pocket and mopped his face. "Then what exactly did you do?"

"I questioned him to try to discover whether his firm had been selling any of the stolen whisky."

"But . . . but why? Why upset him over something that's impossible?"

"Impossible?"

"His firm couldn't do such a thing. Damn it, he's a . . . a gentleman."

"Then I'm glad I'm not."

"You always make things so difficult," moaned Kywood. "Can't you appreciate the fact it's a thousand quid to a penny that all the stolen whisky's in London?"

"I disagree."

"You disagree! Ignoring all the probabilities, you disagree! I'm telling you, Bob, that whisky has been flogged in London."

"No, sir."

"Why d'you say that? Come on, tell me why?"

"One reason is that the hi-jacking was carried out by a local mob, Stretley, Playford, and Finnigan. They were paid somewhere around a thousand quid for the job . . . "

"How d'you know this? You told me nothing about it before. Why do I have . . . "

"We searched Playford's house earlier this evening and found two hundred and sixty-three quid in one-pound notes. That's obviously part of his share of payment. Stretley was boss, so he'd have a bigger cut which makes the total pay-out of the hi-jacking a thousand, or more. If a local seller from here offers stolen whisky in London, he won't get more than ten bob a bottle. That would make his haul worth

146

just over seventeen hundred quid. He's not going to pay out a thousand for the hi-jacking and leave himself with only seven hundred. So he must be selling locally and getting a good price for each bottle."

Kywood fingered his bottom lip. "Who says the centre-man has to be local? Most likely, he's from London. So he sells the whisky in London and can afford a thousand for the hi-jacking."

"A London centre-man would bring down a London mob. In any case, Finnigan's murder proves he's not a Londoner."

"How?"

"The fire in Verlay's Wine Store was started about five in the morning. The candle fuse, judging by the size of the wick that's left, couldn't have burned for more than an hour. Finnigan, then, was put in the cellar around four. No London centre-man would have risked hanging around Fortrow after the hi-jacking just to put Finnigan in the cellar early in the morning. He'd have returned to London as soon as he'd transhipped the whisky and when Finnigan tried to put the black on him he'd have taken Finnigan with him and dumped the body en route or in London."

"How d'you know Finnigan's death is connected with the hi-jacking?"

"Finnigan was . . . "

Kywood interrupted, speaking pugnaciously. "Have you one atom of proof — proof, mark you — that the two things are directly connected?"

"Finnigan was murdered."

"Can you prove conclusively it was a murder?"

"It has to be."

"You've no proof."

"The time fuse . . . "

"A candle left lying about."

"The manager says there were none."

"He's mistaken."

"Why should Finnigan break into the cellar?"

"To pinch some booze."

"But he'd just made himself three hundred quid, or so. Why was the cellar saturated with paraffin?"

"He was setting fire to it to hide the theft."

"He couldn't. He was drugged."

"He was a drug addict, reasonably

competent until he was fool enough to have a drink. If his death wasn't murder, there's nothing to suggest the centre-man isn't a Londoner."

"Finnigan was murdered because he was trying to put the black on the centre-man."

"Prove it," demanded Kywood, more pugnaciously than ever.

"When I told Playford that Finnigan had been murdered, just for a second he was too shocked to think what he was saying. He said: 'When we left him behind . . .' Why did Finnigan stay behind unless it was to discover the identity of the centre-man and blackmail him? Because Finnigan was trying to blackmail, he was murdered, because he was murdered, the centre-man has to be local. Because the centre-man's local, the stolen whisky has to be sold in or around Fortrow."

Kywood shook his head. "It's all ifs. If this, if that, if the other. You've no proof."

"I've proof enough."

"You're twisting facts to suit your theories."

"I'm using the facts to uncover the truth."

"Let's just examine things calmly. You claim the facts prove the whisky's being sold locally. All right, let's agree that for the moment. Then how? Through pubs?"

"No. We've failed to uncover any approach to a pub and in any case there aren't nearly enough pubs in the area to handle the numbers involved. The whisky has to be sold through a firm whose turnover of MacLaren whisky is large enough to absorb the thousands of bottles that were stolen this time and on previous occasions."

"And how many firms in Fortrow are big enough to do that?"

"Only Findren and Sharman."

"Haven't you checked their stocks and records and found precisely nothing? Haven't you had a word with the excise officer and been told he's never discovered a thing wrong? If a . . . "

Kywood stopped talking when Josephine came into the room. She put a tray on which was coffee, sugar, and milk, on the table. "You won't be much longer, will you, Bob?" she said, in a militant tone of voice.

"I wouldn't think so," answered Fusil.

She half turned and spoke directly to

Kywood. "He's working much too hard."

"We all work very hard, Mrs. Fusil," he answered virtuously.

"Do you?" She left and slammed the door shut behind her.

Fusil rightly decided there was nothing he could say to mitigate the effect of his wife's words. He passed a cup of coffee across, then the milk and the sugar. "I want to call in the Fraud Squad, to investigate the books of Sharman and Findren."

"You what?" Kywood, who had been stirring sugar into his coffee, looked at Fusil with an expression of amazement on his face. "Investigate Findren?"

"That's right."

"You must be mad!"

"I don't think so."

"Risk calling in the Fraud Squad because of a load of theories?"

"Because of a number of facts."

"Don't you realise that the borough force has to pay for the services of the Fraud Squad? When the account comes through, it has to be passed by the finance subcommittee of the watch committee. You know as well as me that Findren's chairman of that."

"So?"

Kywood's voice rose. "So have you stopped to think what would happen when the account came through if nothing was turned up and it was clear the money was wasted? Take just one factor involved. Our patrolling P.C.s need more pocket radios, but the finance subcommittee is jibbing at the expense. If we upset Findren any further, he'll see we don't get those radios."

"Then he's no bloody right to be in the position he is," said Fusil bitterly.

"Rights don't always count for much in this world." Kywood's tone of voice became big-brotherly. "Bob, the more senior you get in the force, the more you have to learn about compromise. If you call in the Fraud Squad without the necessary legal proof . . . "

"Which I'm not likely to get until they've carried out their investigations."

Kywood drank his coffee in quick, noisy gulps.

"I want an investigation," said Fusil stubbornly.

"My advice, Bob . . . "

"It's my case."

"I'm trying to help you save yourself from putting your head on the block."

"It'll be my head. Will you put in the request, please."

Kywood did not refuse. If he was careful, all the responsibility for the decision would rest fairly and squarely on Fusil's shoulders should it prove an abortive investigation.

10

A MAN was mugged just outside a dock-side pub and seventy-three pounds were stolen from him; two prostitutes had a savage fight and one was badly injured about the right eye; a gang of thirteen-year-olds wrecked the inside of a kindergarten school; a house was burgled and the two thieves tried vainly to open up the back of a safe with a shutter-cutter — unknown to them, the safe was unlocked; a woman gassed herself because for four years she had had no friends and knew no one in the whole world who gave a damn whether she lived or died; a father had a sudden, wild surge of anger and battered his year-old son because the constant crying scrambled his mind . . .

Fusil struggled to cope with the flood of work and cursed when he failed, as he had to. How many of the general public, he thought despairingly, were aware that crime was on the rampage? How many cared or had the intelligence to know that crime was the bitter enemy of society and when there was too much of it society in its present form must sicken and die?

He left his desk and crossed to the window and looked out. Gone was all the hot sunshine. Today, unbroken cloud, all the same dreary, sodden shade of grey, stretched from horizon to horizon. This, he thought cynically, was the return of the typical English summer.

As he turned, Rowan knocked and entered the room. "I'm just back from the Red Duster Club, sir."

"Any luck?"

"Not really. The doorman's been there for the past eight years. He was telephoned a couple of years back and told there was twenty quid in it for him if he took a message by telephone and passed it on. Since then, he's taken four messages, passed 'em on, and collected eighty quid. He doesn't know who telephoned the messages in or who telephoned to collect 'em."

"How did he get the money?"

"By post. Each time a plain envelope was sent to him at the club with twenty one-pound notes inside it."

"Didn't he notice the postmark?"

"He knows it was London, but can't remember anything more than that."

Fusil tapped on the desk with his fingers. "Obviously, the man has to have visited the club. Can't the doorman suggest who it can be?"

"He swears he's no idea. I reckon he was telling the truth."

After Rowan had gone, Fusil considered what he'd just been told and inevitably came to the conclusion that it didn't add up to a row of beans. The letter with the money was postmarked London, but was that because it had been posted from there as a blind? Or, as Kywood would undoubtedly point out, simply because the centre-man lived in London?

He sat down on the edge of the desk. Were they making any progress in solving the murder and in finding out how the stolen whisky was disposed of? Would the murder be solved without discovering the identity of the centre-man first and being able to prove the identification, which meant the course of the stolen whisky had to be known? Although he was so certain the two were inextricably mixed up, was there still a possibility Finnigan had not been murdered and that all the theories were so much moonshine . . . ? He thumped his fist into the palm of his hand. He was right. He knew it. Even if the proof was not yet to hand. The investigation by the Fraud Squad would prove he was right.

The weather remained wet, windy, and depressing, and the weathermen on television spoke about depressions and cold fronts. Fortrow could become an unfriendly place in summer bad weather. People from nearby coastal resorts came into the town and brought with them an air of bored, resentful aimlessness, shop assistants became bad tempered because customers were so indecisive, the pavements were crowded and the roads became clogged with traffic trying to find parking space. Gangs of youths came down from London and had punch-ups with the locals, seamen became more drunk, more often . . .

Detective Inspector Melchett and Detective Sergeant Price arrived in Fortrow on the ten o'clock from London and were met by a police car which drove them to borough force H.Q. in western division. There, they saw Kywood. Half an hour later, the same police car drove them to eastern divisional H.Q.

Melchett shook hands with Fusil in the latter's room and introduced his sergeant. Fusil rang the desk sergeant and asked him to send someone down to the canteen for three coffees.

"You've had a word with the D.C.I., haven't you?" said Fusil, as he sat down. "Can you tell me what he said?"

"He gave us a general run-down." Melchett was a tall, austere-looking man who spoke with the abrupt manner of someone who never wasted words. "He said there were factors involved here which lay beyond those normally found in a case. I gather the trouble's local politics?"

"It is. I'd strangle all the bloody politicians," said Fusil roughly.

"Another lot would merely crawl out from under the stones," remarked Melchett dryly. "It's Findren whom we have to handle with kid gloves?"

"He wants checking on just as closely as Sharman."

"We'll do our job," said Melchett.

That was one thing for certain, thought Fusil. Melchett had all the appearance of a dour man of conscience, never swayed from the path of duty.

"Mr. Kywood also said that unfortunately our time was necessarily limited," went on Melchett.

"What?" snapped Fusil.

"He carefully explained that our services came a little expensive for the borough funds."

Fusil swore.

"There should be time enough to satisfy ourselves whether anything is not in order. If we uncover something, presumably Mr. Kywood will find it difficult to cut short our further investigations?"

"Never underrate his capabilities," muttered Fusil. He cheered up. "You'll uncover something."

"We will, if it's there. I gather from Mr. Kywood that it's far from certain, though, that the stolen whisky is being shifted down here rather than up in London?"

"That's one of the points on which we differ."

"I see." Melchett smiled briefly. "Perhaps you'll give me a quick run-down on the facts as you know them?"

Fusil, interrupted only when a cadet brought in the coffee, gave a resumé of all the facts regarding the hijacking and the murder.

"I suppose," said Melchett at the conclusion, "you don't mind whether we prove Findren or Sharman the villain, just so long as it's one of them?"

"It'd be worth a month's pay if you could show they'd worked it in collaboration!" Fusil laughed. He was surprised to discover that Melchett had a sense of humour under that desiccated exterior.

The crime figures rose and Fusil worked as hard as he could, sparing neither himself nor those under him. He repeatedly put in requests for help from the uniformed branch and eventually the chief inspector complained to Superintendent Passmore, the divisional superintendent. Passmore was a man of great experience and tact, and he had a courteous manner which masked an inner toughness. He told Fusil that there had never been a D.I. who had as many men as he needed and each D.I. had to work out his own priorities in the light of the man-power available. Fusil accepted the admonition in a reasonably calm manner. He was returning from the superintendent's room when the desk sergeant called out and said Detective Inspector Melchett and his sergeant were waiting for him upstairs. Fusil ran up the stairs, three at a time, to his office.

Melchett greeted him. "The P.C. brought us up and suggested we wait in here — hope you don't mind?"

"Of course not. What's the result?" asked Fusil excitedly.

"Not the one you were hoping for," replied Melchett. "We've discovered nothing suspicious."

Fusil walked round his desk and sat down. He'd been so certain. Time after time, he'd gone through the evidence, time after time he'd come to the same conclusion: one of the two firms had to be selling the stolen whisky. "Did you check everything?"

"Of course — and we've used up every last second of the D.C.I.'s allotted time in order to do so. There are no traces of unexplained whisky in the accounts or the stocks of either firm."

"Surely Sharman, with all those branches he could use to sell the stuff through . . . "

"We've checked the branch figures and stocks against the warehouse figures and stocks and there are no discrepancies, nor are there any signs of unusual sales of whisky at the time of the thefts." Melchett motioned to Price, who passed over a brief-case. Melchett took out a thick bundle of papers which he put on the desk. "These are photostat copies of entries in account books, bank statements, invoices, record cards, suppliers' monthly statements, and so on."

Fusil reached across and picked up the papers. He leafed through them.

Melchett continued to speak in his dry, somewhat toneless voice. "We were obviously looking for discrepancies in stocks or sales figures. We carried out a full stocktaking both at the warehouse and each of the seven shops, taking a number of test counts ourselves. We found virtually no discrepancies whatsoever."

"What precisely does 'virtually' mean?"

"If half a dozen bottles are recorded as smashed, we accept the figure. If our count is half a dozen bottles out on the books, we don't consider that to be of any significance."

"Wasn't there even a hint of unexplained numbers?"

Melchett shook his head as he passed two sheets of foolscap paper across the desk. "I made up a brief abstract to show you the position. You'll see that the number of bottles of MacLaren whisky and the number of bottles of all descriptions sold and the numbers now in stock agree with those in stock two and a half years ago added to all deliveries since then — as recorded by invoices and suppliers' monthly statements."

Figures in quantities always gave Fusil mental indigestion, but Melchett had laid out the figures in a manner that enabled him to follow them without trouble.

"All the accounts are in order," continued Melchett. "The right amounts of money for the stocks received have in every case been remitted from the shops to the warehouse. Cheques paid out from the warehouse to suppliers agree with the accounts due for goods supplied. Bank balances are correct. All cleared cheques match cheque stubs and account books."

"Aren't there any discrepancies?"

"There are only a very few small cheques from the parent company which have not been paid in by the payee — but in any major audit there are always some small cheques that don't, for one reason or another, get put through. I've prepared another summary for you." He passed across three more sheets of foolscap paper.

This time, Fusil found the figures much less easy to follow. He parked the papers to one side. "And it was the same with Findren?"

"Exactly the same, except that Findren was quite unpleasant and far less co-operative than Sharman."

Fusil slumped back in his chair. "Is there any way of selling whisky through a shop and yet not showing it in the books?"

"It becomes a question of quantity. I suppose any shopkeeper can slip some sales through without their being recorded, but we're dealing with thousands of bottles here. No, this number could not be 'lost'. The sales in all the shops show an evenness which is only disturbed by the Christmas trade. In any case, the total yearly sale of any one branch of Sharman of MacLaren whisky is less than the number of bottles of stolen whisky."

"Couldn't the shops be passing off the sales of whisky under the guise of gin, for instance?"

Melchett still spoke patiently. "I mentioned that we checked the sales and stocks of all the liquor handled. There's not the slightest chance the whisky is being sold as something else."

Fusil went to speak, then checked himself.

"To sum up," said Melchett, "we've found nothing suspicious in the accounts or stocks of either of the two firms."

"But the facts all say the whisky has to be sold here." Fusil spoke with angry petulance.

Melchett shook his head. "Unless there's another large firm whose business we haven't checked, it isn't."

"These were the only two that could have handled the quantities involved."

"Then I'm sorry, but that's it." Melchett looked at his watch. "Is there any chance of a car to run us down to the station? We could just catch the twelve o'clock to London."

"I'll take you."

"I don't want to bother you."

"I'll have to carry on from there to report to the D.C.I.," said Fusil.

Melchett spoke sympathetically. "I hope things aren't going to be too rough for you."

Kywood, seated behind his desk, looked up. "You realise, of course, precisely what this means?"

"Naturally," replied Fusil.

"I don't want to labour the point, Bob, but I think you ought to appreciate the full seriousness of the position as it directly affects you."

Kywood, thought Fusil, provided the perfect picture of a smooth bastard of a hypocrite in full action.

"You decided to ignore, or maybe it would be fairer to say overrule, my strong advice not to call in the Fraud Squad. You said that they would inevitably turn up the sale of the stolen whisky, which discovery must identify the centre-man, who had to be the murderer of Finnigan. It hasn't worked out like that, has it?"

"Obviously not."

Kywood's patient expression suggested that

he fully understood the other's belligerence and could even make allowances for it. "The evidence now is that the stolen whisky could not have been sold in Fortrow. This means the centre-man does not live here and there's no proof that Finnigan *was* murdered."

"None of that necessarily follows."

"On the contrary, by your own logic it does."

"Look here, sir, just because . . . "

"Bob, face the facts. You're in a spot and the sooner you realise that, the sooner we can try and find some way of getting you out of it."

"I've done no more than my duty."

"Your duty was to examine all aspects of the case before coming to any final decisions. In the case of the Fraud Squad . . . "

"I wasn't bloody well not going to call them in because of some dirty local politics."

Kywood rested his elbows on the desk and pressed together the tips of the fingers of both hands. "Rightly or wrongly, a man is judged by results. If the best intentions end in the worst results, it's only the results that count." He looked down at the desk, then up again. "It's most unfortunate, but you've been in serious trouble before, haven't you?"

"Yes."

"I know that trouble only came about because you were too keen to arrest a guilty man — but the chief constable is a pragmatist."

"Can't he see a doctor?"

Kywood's voice sharpened. "That sort of attitude doesn't help."

What the hell could help, wondered Fusil with bitter anger? He'd staked everything on an event which had not come to pass. Kywood would always manage to slide out of trouble, so he was left in the sucker's seat. The moral was very clear. Learn to be a politician.

11

THROUGHOUT the latter half of August and the whole of September, the weather remained wet and windy. Then, in the middle of October, long after the last of the holidaymakers had gone from the coastal resorts and the sandy beaches had once more become havens of solitude, there was an Indian summer with warm and sunny days.

Contrary to the normal pattern, crime continued at a level as high as during the mid-summer. In the one week, there were a series of fights in the dock area, some said of racial origin, which culminated in a near-riot in which three men were stabbed, one was slashed close to death with a broken bottle, and at least a score of people received minor injuries. Television showed scenes of the final fight and concentrated on shots of the police defending themselves, which they presented as more evidence of police brutality. There was a bank raid in which a cashier was violently bludgeoned

169

and twenty thousand pounds were stolen: the members of the gang went uncaught. A well-known woman died from an illegal abortion and the man concerned could not be traced. The *Fortrow Gazette* had a leading article, misinformed and badly written, questioning the efficiency of the borough police and pointing out that not even the theft of the whisky had been solved or the death of the man in Verlays Wine Store cleared up.

Fusil, true to character, met the mounting criticism by trying to drive himself and his men still harder than before. Determined to arrest those most concerned in the brutal fight, he gave orders that the inhabitants of every house in the immediate area and the crew of every ship in port should be interrogated.

Braddon tried to object. "Look, sir," he said reasonably, "it's just not on."

"What's not on?" replied Fusil.

"To question all these people, if we don't have anyone else to give us a hand. We're tied up in those other cases as it is. Why can't we ask for help from the county force?"

"You know as well as me. That would

give the county force the excuse to say we can't cope."

"It's true."

"We have to hide the fact," snapped Fusil.

Braddon returned to the general room. "Everything stands," he said. "You do the job as ordered, and without help."

"It's impossible," muttered Rowan.

"All right. Do the impossible."

"But, Sarge . . . "

"There's no arguing. Get out and get started."

Rowan and Welland left the room, but Kerr remained.

"Sarge, today's Saturday," said Kerr.

"Is that supposed to be news?"

"It's my week-end off."

"That's good. That means you're free to give us a hand, doesn't it?"

"I've arranged to go out this afternoon with my fiancée. I promised her . . . "

"Then this will give her the chance to discover you're a liar. Get moving."

Kerr left the general room and went down to the courtyard. He arrived outside just in time to see the C.I.D. Hillman drive out. Friends! he thought bitterly.

A bus took him down town to Dock Road and he entered the docks through number 5 gate. The first ship he boarded was an old, ugly, dirty freighter, flying a Panamanian flag, whose decks were littered with the filthy rubbish of a dock stay. The chief officer spoke a fractured English which became positively shattered when Kerr asked if any members of the crew were known to have been in the fight or bore any signs of personal injury. From the chief officer's cabin, he went below two decks to the crew's quarters. He spoke to a greaser, in oil-stained string vest and cotton trousers, who spoke fluent, if heavily accented, English. According to the greaser, every member of the crew had been aboard on Wednesday evening. He was a liar, thought Kerr dispassionately, but how in the hell was he ever to prove it?

In the course of the next hour, he visited a refrigerated ship unloading carcasses of mutton and crates of butter and a mixed cargo ship that was loading crates and bags of chemical. The crew of the last vessel had all signed on as she was due to sail in two days and meals were being served aboard. Kerr was sharply reminded how hungry he was when he went into the galley. He commented on that fact to the cook and was very fortunate that the other, untypically, was good natured and generous. He served Kerr a huge portion of steak and kidney pie and afterwards offered apple tart.

When Kerr walked down the gangway, he was fairly certain he had eaten too much. Perhaps, he thought, he should have refused that second helping of apple tart but it really had been delicious. He went to the end of the berth and began to walk along the main dock road and had just crossed the railway lines when there was the tooting of a car's horn. Welland, at the wheel of the C.I.D. Hillman, came alongside and braked to a halt. "Have you had any luck?" asked Welland.

"I've just had a damned good lunch."

"I'm talking about the job."

Kerr shrugged his shoulders. "What do you think? No one saw anything, heard anything, or knows anything."

"And even if anyone did, he's not going to be fool enough to say so." Welland spoke with unusual pessimism since even his buoyant nature was not proof against working on and on at a job which had such little chance of being successful. "What a lousy way to spend a Saturday afternoon."

Kerr leaned against the driving door. "It was meant to be my week-end off and I'd promised to go up into the Keighley Hills with Helen. She loves it up there says that when we win the pools, that's where we'll go to live. She hasn't got a 'phone at home so I can't ring up to say what's happened — she's always getting on to me for not letting her know when I can't turn up as I said I would."

"You'll cop it, then, and no mistake."

"That's for sure," said Kerr gloomily. He stared resentfully at the bonnet of the Hillman and was just thinking that the patch of rust was growing in size when his mind was suddenly excited by an idea. "Parry — how long d'you reckon it's going to take us to cover all the ships and dock-side houses?"

"All week-end. Maybe longer."

"Then no one can say a quick couple of hours is vital. Be a pal and let me have the car for a short time."

"What are you going to do with it?"

"Nip off to Helen and explain what's

happened. And maybe just go for a quick drive into the hills."

"You must be nuts. If old Fusil caught you doing that, he'd rip your liver out and fry it in front of your eyes."

"He'll never know. In any case, we're wasting our time here. Be a real sport."

"You can't be serious?"

"Look, what harm can it do? Come to that, I'll keep going a bit longer tonight and make up my time. What could be more honest than that?" He opened the driving door.

Welland hesitated and then stepped out on to the road. "You're being a right mug," he said seriously. "No fooling, if you get caught you're liable to be chopped out of the force."

Kerr sat back behind the wheel. "How's anyone going to know? Fusil's back at the station and staying there, Braddon said he wasn't coming down this way until late afternoon. Even if someone starts shouting for me, with all the ships to choose from, they'll never be able to prove I'm not around. In any case, it's my week-end off."

"Don't you think . . . " began Welland.

"I'm off." Kerr engaged first gear and accelerated away. One small part of his mind was trying to tell him that what he was doing *was* stupid, and he wanted to stifle such a thought before it had time to dissuade him.

At the gates, a dock policeman waved him to a stop. "Come on, mate, you know you don't just drive straight through. What's the hurry?"

"I'm trying to rush two thousand fags and a keg of brandy through," said Kerr.

"Now just you . . . "

"Keep your shirt on." Kerr showed his warrant card.

"You blokes from the borough force are real bright and breezy, aren't you?" muttered the policeman, ill-temperedly.

Kerr drove out. His conscience became more active, but he assured himself that if this had been an important case he would never have dreamed of sloping off. This investigation, occasioned really by the T.V. coverage, was doomed to failure as anyone with an ounce of common sense could see. His temporary absence couldn't possibly have any effect.

He told Helen he would have to get

back fairly smartly because a lot of work had come in suddenly, but Fusil had said he could be away for a couple of hours.

Keighley Hills possessed a rolling beauty that had somehow almost escaped being built on: only one line of super-pylons and one tall T.V. relay mast broke their skyline. Woods dotted their crowns and often reached down into the valleys, while in the valleys were farms whose houses and outbuildings were centuries old and had become part of the landscape. From the southernmost hills, there were views across to the sea.

The sunshine still held enough warmth for Helen and Kerr to spread out a rug to sit on whilst they had tea.

"John, you're hardly eating," she said suddenly. "Is something wrong with you?"

"I'm as fit as a fiddle."

"But there's apricot jam in that sandwich — I thought you loved it?"

"I do. But . . . Well as a matter of fact, I had rather an enormous lunch."

"When you knew we were having tea together?"

"I didn't . . . I mean I . . . " He stopped when he saw she was smiling, enjoying the pleasant intimacy of pulling his leg. "When did I last tell you you were lovely?" he asked softly.

"Not for ages and ages."

He took hold of her hand. "Why are you going to marry me, darling?"

"I can't think," she said contentedly, as she leaned against him.

"Is it because I'm so handsome and witty?"

"John Kerr, you know just what I think of you when you get smug and self-satisfied like that!" She sat upright. "Come on, eat up that sandwich."

"Yes, ma'am. Tell me, are you going to order me around all the time when we're married?"

"Of course. But you won't realise it."

"Fred says that's the way all women work."

"He would, if you mean Fred Rowan. D'you know, John, I always feel sorry for him — but I just can't get to like him." She stared out to sea, a greeny blue and divided into two by a shaft of sunlight.

"You do know he leads a hell of a life? He's never certain what his wife's up to."

"Why isn't he?" She suddenly spoke

with urgency. "How can a marriage reach such a state? He and his wife must have trusted each other absolutely when they got married."

"I don't know," he said slowly and thoughtfully. "These things just seem to happen. I got called last week to a house in which a woman had been so badly beaten up by her husband she had to go off to hospital. The odd thing is, she wouldn't tell me anything when I wanted a statement."

"She was still a wife." Helen seemed to shiver. "Let's change the subject. I hate talking about the miserable things in life." She poured him out a cup of tea from a Thermos flask and added milk from a bottle. "When are we going to get married?"

"Tomorrow morning."

"Don't be silly."

"What's so silly about that?" he protested.

"Only the impossibility. I just wish we could — I've never longed for anything so much." She had a warm, loving nature that emotionally gave generously. Her loyalty to him would never waver. She was not beautiful in the conventional sense, yet her character was beautiful and he had had the luck and wit to discover this.

When he'd finished the tea, he had a quick look at his watch: twenty to four. Even if they left immediately, he wouldn't be back at the docks by four o'clock. Suppose Fusil didn't stay at the station, suppose Braddon decided to have an earlier look round the docks . . .

"Is it time we were moving?" she asked.

"I think perhaps we ought to." He threw the dregs from the cup on to the grass, stood up, then held out his hand and helped her to her feet.

She packed the uneaten sandwiches, buns, and cake, and put them together with the Thermos and bottle of milk into the cane shopping basket.

Just before he started the engine, he said: "What's the quickest way back? The way we came?"

"I'd have thought it would be quicker to cut over the hills and past the old quarry."

He nodded. "I guess you're right. Let's give it a try, then."

The way was a narrow lane that crossed the line of the hills, going up and down like a switchback. When clear it was the quicker route, but the narrowness of the lane meant that any traffic caused a hold-up. For a couple of minutes they were behind a heavy lorry that belched out clouds of black exhaust smoke, then they no sooner squeezed past than they came up to a tractor drawing a trailer-load of straw.

Kerr once again checked on the time. Just after four. Silently, he cursed — why did one always meet the slowest possible vehicles when one was in the most tearing hurry? Fusil was so flaming sharp he might well make a special, unscheduled trip down to the docks to see that the investigations were being properly carried out on this sunny Saturday afternoon. The D.I. had a habit of demolishing excuses, alibis, and protestations of innocence . . .

She interrupted his galloping thoughts. "You're worried about something." She turned until she could study his face.

"Only about how to get past this dozy tractor driver this side of Christmas."

"I'm sure it's more than that because you've been on edge from the moment you noticed the time when we were picnicking.

Are you supposed to be here at all?"

"Of course I am," he protested loudly. "It's just that I told Fusil I'd be back as soon after four as possible." How the hell had she hit on the truth? he wondered. What was it going to be like when they were married? If he sneaked away for a couple of pints with the boys, was she going to know all about it even before he lifted his elbow for the first time? He blew the car's horn. The tractor and trailer did not deviate from their central course. Right now, Fusil might well be stamping up and down the docks, explaining in detail what he was going to do when he laid his hands on a certain D.C. A drumhead court-martial. The station P.C.s lined up in serried ranks. Truncheons reversed. A roll of drums. John Kerr led out under close escort. The lapels of his jacket torn off . . .

"Wake up," she said. "You can get by now."

He realised they had reached the crest of the hill and the lane had widened until he could get by. He dropped down into third and accelerated. After a while, the tired engine of the Hillman responded and they passed the trailer and tractor.

The lane began to wind downhill, between tree-covered banks, and at the foot of the hill they passed a dilapidated broken wooden notice which said Horniton Quarry was a hundred yards ahead. Someone had told him that the quarry had closed down five years ago, after keeping one family wealthy for over sixty-five years — some people had all the luck. The entrance on to the road was twenty feet wide, whilst set ten feet back were rusty metal gates and a chain-link fence that was half down. A car was parked in the gateway, bonnet outwards, and a man stood by the driving door. As the Hillman came abreast of the entrance, the man turned and Kerr caught a quick glimpse of his face.

Kerr drove round the next corner, then slowed down until the car was barely moving.

"Has something gone wrong with the car?" asked Helen.

"No," he answered. "It's just that I'm trying to work out who that bloke was by the car at the quarry. I'm sure his face was familiar, but I'm damned if I can put a name to it."

"But what does it matter who he is? I thought you were in a hurry to get back? Look, John, if you're not supposed to be here at all, it's no good going along at this speed, is it?"

"I suppose you're right," he said. He changed gear, accelerated, changed into third and had almost reached a bend in the road when he suddenly braked so harshly that she was almost thrown against the dashboard. "Of course! It was Ginger Playford, that's who it was!"

"Next time you're going to stop like that, you might just give me warning," she complained, with good reason.

"I'm sorry." He spoke excitedly. "He's one of the blokes who was mixed up in the hi-jacking of the whisky lorry. What the hell's he doing parked back there in the quarry. And that looked like a Jaguar, pretty new."

"Why can't he have come out just for the ride? You must get back . . ."

"Villains like him don't go for rides in the countryside. And why park in a disused quarry? And where would he have got a spanking Jaguar from if he hadn't nicked it?"

"John . . . "

He interrupted her. "I'm going back to discover if he's up to something."

"Not on your own," she cried.

"If he is on a job, he won't stay around long enough for anyone else to get here in time to give me a hand."

She wanted desperately to argue, to make him eschew taking such a risk, but knew she must say nothing. He had a duty to do. Therefore, she had a duty to let him do it, no matter how wild her thoughts.

He turned the car in two locks and drove back round the corner. They came in sight of the quarry entrance. The Jaguar was still parked, but Playford was now sitting behind the wheel. Kerr swung the Hillman into the entrance and stopped it so that the Jaguar was boxed-in. "Get behind the wheel," he said tersely. "If there's any trouble, drive like hell out of it and call for help."

"John . . . "

"Just do that."

He left the Hillman and walked towards the Jaguar. Playford's expression made it quite clear that something was up.

There was the sound of feet, crunching

on the gravel roadway that wound round to the right inside the quarry. Two men, wearing overalls and caps, came into view. When they saw him, they stopped suddenly. He identified one of them as Stretley, but did not know the other.

Playford slammed open the door of the Jaguar and scrambled out on to the roadway. "It's a split," he shouted wildly. He threw himself forward at Kerr. Kerr sidestepped and kicked out with his right foot: he caught Playford and sent him crashing to the ground.

Stretley and the third man came forward together. Kerr ducked one blow, but received another to the side of his neck. He hit Stretley across the face with the edge of his right hand. In the momentary pause that followed, he looked back at the Hillman and saw with violent despair that Helen was not driving off as he had told her to.

He used his fists, knees, feet, and even his teeth. In such a fight, the man who observed the Queensberry Rules was a dead duck. Fingers gripped his throat, trying to throttle him, digging brutally into his flesh, crushing shut his windpipe. He swung both hands up between the other's arms and then outwards and forced the fingers away from his throat. In doing this, he'd left his stomach unprotected: a fist crashed into it, doubling him up. A boot thudded into the side of his right buttock and he fell. He rolled over. Another boot crashed down into the dirt, exactly where the centre of his head would have been. As he tried to come to his feet, they rushed him and bowled him over. He caught one leg and twisted and the man fell awkwardly to the ground, raising a puff of dust. A shoe raked his shoulder and slid off to hit his head, momentarily sending his senses reeling. Despair washed across his mind. He hadn't a chance. He tried again to get to his feet because if he stayed on the ground he was done for. He managed to reach a kneeling position before they hurled him back to the ground. He was kicked on the right kneecap and the pain was immediate and sickening. He rolled sideways, grabbed a leg, and bit into the flesh and there was a wild shout: another kick thudded into his side. He could feel the strength deserting him. In a strangely detached way, he knew his fight was nearly over. There was some fear within him, but there was also a bitter anger that his body should prove so weak.

In the car, Helen had watched the brutal, vicious struggle with such a sense of outraged shock that the reality of it was almost destroyed. But when she saw John on the ground, frantically trying to avoid being stamped and kicked to death, the ghastly reality of the scene abruptly became overwhelming. John had ordered her to drive off for help, but no help that she could summon would arrive in time to save him. She dreaded all violence, yet never hesitated. She grabbed the bottle of milk from the picnic basket, ran to the struggling bunch of men, and swung the bottle with all her strength. She had played hockey at school and still possessed a strong right arm. The bottle smashed across Stretley's cheekbone and he screamed, like a wounded hare, then staggered away, hands clasped to his face. The bottle broke, spraying milk everywhere, and she was left with just the neck and a long triangle of glass. She stabbed at the nearest man with this and the glass sliced through his coat and shirt into the flesh of his right arm. As the pain flashed through his arm, he stared down at the torn and bloody coat in dazed surprise.

Kerr was not immediately aware of what had happened. All he knew was that suddenly he was faced by only one man. He brought up his knee and caught the other in the groin. Playford collapsed to the ground and began to retch.

Kerr struggled to his feet. He stared at Helen and saw the neck of the shattered bottle in her hand. For a few seconds she did not move, then she began to cry. By the time he had gathered her into his arms, she was sobbing so violently that her whole body shook.

The third man, right arm dripping blood, staggered across to the Jaguar and struggled to open the driving door, all his actions clumsy because he was having to use his left hand. Kerr released Helen and ran over to the Jaguar. The third man frantically shouted he wasn't giving any more trouble. Kerr clubbed him with fist and boot, not really aware of what he was doing. He was suffering terror at the thought of what could have happened to Helen.

12

FUSIL looked away from the blackness of the night at his watch. The luminous hands showed it was after eight. He stared back into the night. A hundred yards nearer the empty corrugated-iron sheds of the quarry was the hi-jacked lorry and in position at strategic points around the lorry were Braddon, Welland, and five unformed P.C.s. Three patrol cars were standing by in a half-mile circle, ready to block off all exits to the lane outside.

For how much longer would there be any point to waiting? Surely, the centre-man would have intended to drive the lorry away as soon as Stretley and his mob had left? Probably, he'd been hidden in the vicinity and had seen or heard the fight and realised the job was blown, so had vanished. But, there was just the chance he had decided not to collect the lorry until much later — so therefore, the watch must continue.

Fusil took his empty pipe from his

pocket and put it in his mouth. This time, they were really going to get somewhere. They'd landed Stretley, Playford, and a villain called Hobbs and these three were going to help prove that Detective Inspector Fusil had been right from the beginning.

It was strange how black night really was: living in a town one forgot. He shuffled his way over to the car and sat down in the driving seat. He closed the door carefully and there was only the smallest of clicks. He called up H.Q. on the radio and asked if there was any news on D.C. Kerr or Miss Barley? The duty inspector said that they had at last heard from Fortrow. D.C. Kerr had sustained heavy bruising, but no broken bones and no internal injuries. Miss Barley was suffering from shock, but nothing worse.

Fusil, sitting behind his desk, studied Kerr. The morning light was weak, because of the heavily overcast sky, but the bruise on Kerr's cheek stood out sharply. "Where were you at four o'clock yesterday afternoon?" asked Fusil, his voice sharp.

Kerr stared at a fixed spot on the

far wall. He heard the bells of Fortrow cathedral and it reminded him that today was Sunday. He rubbed his knee-cap, which still ached.

"Were you down at the docks?"

"No, sir."

"Then where were you?"

"Having a picnic in the Keighley Hills, sir," muttered Kerr reluctantly.

"You disobeyed orders and deserted your duties?"

"Yes."

"You know the penalties of such incredible and utterly senseless action?"

Kerr did not answer.

Fusil began to fill his pipe with tobacco. "You're a right lucky idiot," he said conversationally, his voice no longer sharp. "Normally, you'd be returned to the uniform branch or be chucked out of the force for that sort of stupidity. As it is, I'm called on to congratulate you."

Kerr relaxed.

"What's more, I'd very much like the chance to tell Miss Barley exactly what I think of her pluck. D'you think she's fit enough to join you in having a drink with my wife and me this evening?"

"I'm sure she is, sir," said Kerr.

"That's fixed, then. I'll give you the time later."

Kerr thought the interview was at an end and turned to go. Fusil spoke again. "Kerr, just remember one thing. Any man who deserts his job to go on a picnic is a goddamn fool, whatever the results."

Kerr turned back and faced the desk. He spoke quietly. "If I hadn't gone for that picnic, sir, we'd not have Stretley, Playford, Hobbs, and the whisky."

"A moralist would no doubt be able to convince you of the falsity of the equation, I can't. I'm just trying to drive it home into that thick head of yours that a bloke only has the luck to get away with what you have once in a lifetime."

"I won't forget that, sir."

Fusil lit his pipe. Kerr had acted foolhardily, which was in character, but had got away with it because he was very lucky. If there was one factor which signalled out a man for success, it was luck. With luck, a man reached the top. Kerr had the ability, the intelligence, the persistence, to make the high ranks in the force: if luck stayed with him and age stripped away the foolhardiness, that's where he'd end up.

Fusil stared at the smoke as it curled its way upwards, suddenly to be swirled apart by a draught. Could he consider himself lucky? Would it take him to the top ranks, where he so passionately longed to be? In the past, luck had occasionally deserted him: yet at other times it had stayed with him when he'd taken risks that would horrify many more conventionally minded members of the force.

The telephone rang. The police doctor, speaking from the general hospital, said that Stretley was now fit enough to be interrogated, but that the other two were still too ill. Fusil thanked the doctor and then asked if he could speak to the sergeant who, together with a P.C., was keeping watch on the three men. He told the sergeant to bring Stretley to the station and leave the P.C. on watch at the hospital.

As he replaced the receiver, Fusil recalled the last glimpse he had had of Hobbs last night. Hobbs had looked as if he'd been beaten up by an expert. Fusil hadn't asked questions, but knew quite well what had happened. Kerr had been wild with fear of what might have happened to his fiancée

194

and had worked out that fear on Hobbs. In similar circumstances he, Fusil, would have done the same thing. If any villain tried to harm Josephine, he'd kill the bastard.

Stretley was brought into the station at eleven-thirty and taken to one of the interview rooms. When his arrival was reported, Fusil picked up a folder from his desk and went down. He told the sergeant, who had brought Stretley from the hospital, to leave. He wanted no witnesses from the uniformed branch present at this interview.

He sat down opposite Stretley at the scarred wooden table and opened the folder, took out several sheets of typewritten paper, and stacked them neatly on one side. He slid out a ball-point pen from his inside coat pocket. Only then did he bother to look at Stretley.

Stretley's left cheek was heavily dressed and a dark, angry bruise spread out from under the dressing to the base of his eye. Fusil spoke casually. "You know something? You ought to stay away from fighting women. Stick to punks in your own class."

"That goddamn bitch near smashed my face up," muttered Stretley.

"They tell me she has a fine right-arm action."

Stretley cursed.

"Still, you're better off than the other two. Hobbs is going to take a long time to get back to normal — broken bones and things — and Playford got belted so hard in his family jewels that he may never be the same man again."

"The split was tryin' to kill Joe," said Stretley viciously. "Joe was shoutin' 'e weren't goin' to do nothing, but the split went on and on."

"My report says that Hobbs fought savagely to avoid arrest and my officer had the greatest difficulty in subduing him."

"That's a bleeding lie. Joe 'ad given up, but that bastard went on kicking and 'itting 'im. 'E was going to murder Joe."

"How very dramatic," said Fusil, in a bored voice. He turned over one of the sheets of paper. "Back at the end of July you, Playford, and Finnigan nicked a load of whisky from the lorry-park at the Jack of Hearts."

"I ain't nicked nothing." Stretley assumed

a look of studied blankness.

"You dressed as repair mechanics, broke into the cab of the lorry, and drove it off and up to the hills. You and Playford cleared off, but Finnigan stayed behind to try and put the black on the centre-man who came to collect the whisky."

"You're joking."

"Since Finnigan acted so stupidly, how come you were given the job this time of nicking the lorry?"

"What lorry?"

"Have a guess."

"I don't know nothing about no lorry."

"Going blind? It was parked slap in the middle of the road just past the bend."

"You can't prove nothing."

Fusil smiled, in a pitying kind of way.

Stretley fingered the dressing on his cheek.

"I don't want to make things too difficult for you," said Fusil, "so I'll just tell you that we found a strand of material caught up on the cab seat of the lorry and we've matched it against the material in the overalls Hobbs was wearing."

"You couldn't've done," said Stretley,

but he did not manage to sound confident.

"Another thing, there was a patch of damp soil by the side of the cab and this recorded a shoe pattern. Your shoe pattern."

Instinctively, Stretley looked down at his shoe. He jerked his gaze away. "It weren't my shoe."

"Didn't the sergeant at the hospital tell you that we borrowed your shoe for a time?"

"You're trying to fix me," shouted Stretley.

"No need. You've fixed yourself." Fusil sat back. "How much were you to be paid for the job this time — same as before?"

"I ain't done no job."

Fusil picked up a pencil and began to doodle on the sheet of paper in front of himself. He shaded in a circle, then looked up. "With the kind of form you've got, I suppose the courts will give you three or four years for nicking the lorry."

"I didn't nick nothing."

"For assaulting my D.C., they'll add on another three or four years."

"Assault 'im. We didn't do no assaulting. We come round the corner and 'e's punching-up Ginger. All we did was to try to 'elp Ginger."

"And for assaulting his fiancée, they'll add on anything up to another seven or eight. Even in today's permissive society, judges don't like women being assaulted."

"We didn't assault 'er," shouted Stretley, his voice filled with bitter anger. "She came at us with that bottle. We didn't know nothing 'til then."

"How very unfair."

"It's all right for you to laugh." Stretley again fingered the dressing on his cheek.

"I'm not laughing," said Fusil, and grinned.

"I'm telling you, we didn't know nothing about 'er 'til she went for us."

"That's not the evidence my D.C. will give in court."

"But if she'd stayed in the car, we wouldn't 'ave touched 'er."

"How unlucky for you she didn't do just that. I told you at the beginning, you jumped out of your class."

"You bleeding well know 'ow it was: you know we didn't go for 'er."

Fusil was silent.

"I wants a smoke," said Stretley suddenly.

Fusil shrugged his shoulders. "I never use cigarettes."

"Get us some."

Fusil made no answer.

"Look, Mister, what's it you want?"

"Facts."

"I've told the facts. We didn't assault 'er."

"You'll never be believed."

"It's the truth."

"That adds to the irony, but not to your chances."

Stretley chewed at his lower lip. "What d'you want?" he demanded for the second time.

"I've just told you: facts."

"Suppose . . . Suppose I talks?"

"If you're really helpful, I might be able to persuade my D.C. and his fiancée not to press their allegations of assault."

"You're trying to put the black on me."

"Never," said Fusil.

Stretley searched his pockets for a cigarette, even though he knew he had none. He fiddled with the middle button of his coat, twisting it first one way, then the other.

"D'you feel like telling me about this

job and all the others?" asked Fusil. "Or would you rather go down for a ten-year stretch?"

Stretley said: "I need a smoke."

Fusil called in the uniformed constable who had relieved the sergeant outside. "Have you got a fag, lad?"

"Yes, sir." The P.C. took a pack from his pocket. He handed it over.

"Thanks." Fusil extracted a cigarette and rolled it across the table. He handed the pack back to the P.C. and said: "You'd better stay in here and take some notes." The P.C. walked over to a chair against the far wall and sat down. Stretley lit the cigarette which he had picked up and drew the smoke deep into his lungs.

"Shall we begin at the beginning?" said Fusil calmly, but with a snap to his voice which could not be missed.

"I got 'phoned up," said Stretley. He stopped.

"Well?"

"A bloke offered me a grand for doing a job."

"Who was he?"

"I don't know."

"You'll have to do better than that."

"I tell you, I don't know. 'E just 'phoned."

"You'll have asked questions?"

"I didn't get no answers."

"You wouldn't have done the job in those circumstances."

"I didn't 'ave no choice. I was skint and owed money to the boys and they was wanting payment. I needed a share of that grand. The bloke said I could do the job 'ow I liked. All 'e'd do was tell me when the lorry would be along."

"Did you do the earlier hi-jackings?"

Stretley drew on the cigarette. He stared at the door, then quickly at Fusil, then down at the table "Yes," he muttered.

"O.K. Let's talk about July. What happened to Finnigan?"

"Ed was a stupid bastard." Stretley spoke bitterly. "Wasn't content with 'is fair cut. Said we ought to find out 'oo was collecting the lorry and put on the black. I tried to argue 'im out of it, but 'e wouldn't listen. 'E stayed with the lorry. I don't know nothing more."

"Who killed him?"

"I don't know."

"The centre-man must have got on to you after the job?"

" 'E got on the 'phone and wanted to know why Ed stayed behind. I said Ed was a stupid bastard."

"Did he say what had happened to Finnigan?"

"No."

"Did you ask him?"

"No."

"Was this after you'd been questioned by us?"

Stretley nodded.

"Where does the centre-man 'phone you from?"

"I don't know."

"A call-box?"

"I tell you, I don't know."

"Does the call come through an operator?"

"No."

"What's his voice like?"

"Ordinary."

"You're not telling me much," said Fusil.

"I'm telling you all I know," muttered Stretley.

Was he, wondered Fusil, making a full confession, or was he holding back some vital piece of information? Fusil unwillingly came to the first conclusion.

Stretley's one aim and object now was to save his own skin.

Fusil telephoned Kywood's house immediately after lunch.

"That was a neat bit of work on the part of your D.C.," said Kywood.

"Yes, sir, it was." What would Kywood say, wondered Fusil, if he knew Kerr had only caught the three villains because he'd deserted his job? Kywood's mind would work itself into knots trying to find the proper and prescribed way in which to view such events.

"Well, what have you learned from the interview? Cleared the whole thing up, eh?"

Fusil gave the other a carefully edited version of the morning's interview of Stretley.

"Oh!" said Kywood. "Not so good, is it? You haven't made the progress you told us we would."

"I only said I hoped."

"Comes to the same thing, doesn't it, from a practical point of view? I assured the chief constable that everything was wrapped up."

"Tell him the paper burst."

"What's that?"

"Nothing, sir."

"Look, Bob, this is real important. You've got to start getting somewhere."

"It's not all loss, sir. We've had positive confirmation now that the centre-man's local."

"You can't say that when Stretley makes out he doesn't know who he is."

"Stretley has confirmed he was paid a thousand pounds each time to organise the hi-jackings."

"Well?"

"I pointed out before, the centre-man could only afford a thousand if the whisky is sold locally." Fusil tried to speak patiently. "There's another fact. Finnigan tried to put the black on the centre-man last time, yet Stretley was still used for this job. Why? A London centre-man would move to a new mob at once. Either our centre-man doesn't know any other mobs, or he can't open up any channels of communication with another one and still stay out of sight, or he's a special reason for carrying on with Stretley."

"What could that be?"

"To prove to himself that he's so goddamn clever he can risk using Stretley again and get away with it."

"I don't understand," protested Kywood.

You might, thought Fusil, given enough time.

Kywood said he hoped Fusil would soon sort things out to the satisfaction of the chief constable and rang off.

Fusil paced his office. He'd spoken confidently enough, but was he justified? He'd said that events again proved the centre-man was local, which in turn meant the whisky was being sold locally. But only two firms could shift large amounts of stolen whisky and they'd both been investigated and cleared. He'd said the centre-man was trying to prove to himself how very clever he was, but was that the only explanation of why Stretley was used again to carry out the hi-jackings?

13

JOSEPHINE had roasted a leg of lamb for supper, which they ate half an hour after Helen and Kerr had left. Fusil had two helpings of that, together with roast potatoes and peas, and then went on to have two helpings of the sherry trifle that followed.

As he finished, she smiled fondly at him. "You've had a really good meal, Bob."

"I was pretty hungry, I don't mind admitting. I forgot to have any tea."

"How on earth could you do that? I thought the internal alarm clock in your tummy never let you down."

He yawned. "I've spent all day tied up with the Stretley mob."

She lit a cigarette. "Ever since they've left, I've been thinking of Helen and what could have happened to her. It makes me go all cold inside."

He nodded. "I know. And yet even now she doesn't seem to realise just how lucky she was — which is as well from her point of view, I suppose."

"She's going to make a wonderful wife. Young John Kerr couldn't have chosen anyone nicer."

"I rather think she chose him and he had the good sense to go along with her choice."

"Stop being cynical."

"I'm not. He was always chasing fresh pastures until he suddenly learned life could be brutal. When that happened, she was waiting to pick up the pieces." He yawned again, then stood up. "I'm going into the study for a spell."

"Must you?" She looked up at him, frowning slightly. "Why can't you take the rest of the evening off? After all, it is Sunday."

"Josey, I'll swear black and blue that Stretley's evidence confirms the centre-man is local and the whisky is being sold locally, right under my nose. It's ten to one the centre-man is Sharman, simply because of the outlets for the stolen whisky that he controls. But his accounts and stocks were checked and I was told he couldn't possibly be handling the whisky. So?" He shrugged his shoulders. "So what's the answer to the riddle? I've got to find it."

She went to speak, but checked herself. She knew he had been telling the truth: he *had* to find the answer to the riddle, no matter how many times in the past he had tried and failed, not simply because that was what police work was all about, but because he must prove to himself he was right. Sometimes, she wished that he didn't need always to prove himself — surely this overwhelming need suggested some sort of weakness of character? — but he would never change. In any case, if he were different in character, could he be the same man she loved so deeply and passionately?

Fusil left the kitchen and went through the hall to his study. It was tiny, designated by the architect a boxroom, and although the desk was very small it left little space for anything else. He squeezed past the desk and sat down in the cane chair. He lit his pipe and began to fill the place with acrid smoke.

On the desk, spread out in a rough semi-circle, were papers dealing with the Finnigan murder, the July hijacking of the lorry, the subsequent enquiries, and all the photostat copies of accounts and stocks which Melchett had left him. However many times had he waded through this lot, trying to find something he had missed which would lead him to the truth?

He leaned back in the chair. This case, just as any other, rested on personalities because crime was committed by persons. On the face of things, Sharman had to be in the clear — no trace of the stolen whisky had been found, either in the shops or the warehouse or as unexplained figures in his accounts. But Sharman had been jeering at him when he visited the warehouse, just as he had been jeering at Kerr on Kerr's first visit there. Why? Was it the contempt of a self-made man for someone who hadn't reached success in life — when success was measured by money? Was it the amused contempt of the innocent man who watched the floundering attempts of the bucolic police who hadn't enough sense even to know when a man just had to be innocent? Was it the superior contempt of a very clever man watching the floundering efforts of the bucolic police, knowing they could suspect all they liked but they'd never find out? Wasn't the man who again employed Stretley for this last hi-jacking either a fool or someone who was quite certain of his superior cleverness and determined to prove it?

Fusil fingered the thick pile of photostat pages. The figures failed to show any discrepancies in money or stocks. Ten thousand pounds' worth of whisky had been stolen from the Jack of Hearts, roughly as much again on each of the previous hi-jackings, yet the accounts at no time showed ten thousand pounds unaccounted for and the stocks held no extra three thousand five hundred-odd bottles of whisky. He suddenly slammed his fist down on the desk. There were no discrepancies, yet for him to be right there had to be.

He leafed through the pages. Figures, figures, figures: enough to give him mental constipation for months. He came to the bank statements. Some of the cheques were for thousands of pounds: he'd never signed a cheque for a thousand in his life. At times, in one of the accounts, there was an overdraft of five figures: he'd once inadvertently overdrawn his account by twenty-five pounds and the bank manager had raised all hell. Only the rich could afford to borrow. There was an entry in pencil on the page he was looking at. Puzzled by it for a moment, he remembered Melchett telling him that one or two small cheques had not been paid in — something quite in the normal course of events. How blasé could you get, wondered Fusil? He'd certainly never not paid in a cheque someone had given him!

He leafed through the rest of the statements, knowing from bitter experience they would tell him nothing — yet he had to do something to suggest to himself that he was taking meaningful action. There were more cheques for thousands of pounds. How did the ordinary person afford to drink all the liquor that this money represented? There were more large overdrafts. People said it was easier to get an overdraft for ten thousand than a hundred. More small cheques drawn but not paid in.

He turned over the last of the bank statements and came to the stock reconciliation sheets which Melchett had said showed there were not now, and never had been, any unexplained quantity of bottles in stock. How did anyone make sense of these endless columns of figures?

After the reconciliation sheets, there were all the cheque stubs and after them . . . He slumped back in the chair. God, he was tired! So tired, that he was having trouble in focussing his eyes and his eyelids kept drooping down.

He stood up, turned, and opened the window. The air was cold and damp, but it did wake him slightly. He looked at his watch: a quarter to ten. If he had any sense, he'd say to hell with everything and go up to bed. Melchett had said there was no fiddle, so what could be the point in staring at figures which he didn't understand? Yet there was one fact he could not forget — Sharman had been jeering at him and wasn't the continued employment of Stretley an extension of this satisfied contempt?

He shut the window, returned to the desk, sat down, and stubbornly stared at the pile of papers. His eyelids became heavier than ever. A pain began behind his eyes.

Josephine entered the room. "Bob, it's time you went up to bed."

Perversely, he said: "I can't yet."

"You look three parts asleep."

"Get me a cup of black coffee, love, and skip the lecture."

She reached across the desk and fondled his right cheek. "Sometimes, I'd like to kick you where it really hurts — just to knock some sense into you." She went out.

His eyes closed. How many of his fellow D.I.s would still be struggling with the case? Wouldn't they have had the sense to accept the fact that once Sharman and Findren had been cleared the only possibility left was that the stolen whisky had to have been sold in London? Wouldn't they have called Finnigan's death a death by misadventure in furtherance of a theft and have removed it from the crime list? Wouldn't they have side-stepped trouble . . . He fell asleep for a few seconds.

He jerked awake. The truth must be somewhere. All detectives were taught that: "Every crime leaves traces, but these are not always directly recognisable so that every inconsistency and every discrepancy must be minutely examined, however remote or insignificant it may seem." Hadn't he investigated every discrepancy and inconsistency and discovered nothing? He fell asleep again.

He woke up, mentally convinced he had been asleep for hours. A quick look at his watch showed him he was wrong. He began to collect up all the papers, hoping physical movement would keep sleep away. He noticed on one of the bank statements the pencilled-in amount of thirty-five shillings for one of the cheques which had not been paid in. Here was one of the discrepancies in the case. Cheque number 247562 for thirty-five shillings. When you were searching for an extra ten thousand pounds, you had to be pretty far gone to think that the discrepancy of thirty-five shillings could be of the slightest significance.

He stacked up the rest of the statements and as he squared them up he noticed the top one also had pencilled in a cheque which had not been paid in. Number 446792 for three pounds fifteen-shillings and four-pence. Why the hell wasn't there a cheque for ten thousand that shouldn't be there?

Josephine came into the room and put

a cup of coffee on the desk. "It's sugared. I'm going to bed, Bob. Please don't be too long."

"I won't," he answered, without conviction. She sighed, then left.

He drank some coffee, replaced the cup on the saucer, and fell asleep. In the short time he stayed asleep, he had a vivid dream of which he had no memory when he awoke other than it had been.

Something was niggling his mind. He tried to make out what, couldn't, and shrugged his shoulders. He drank the rest of the coffee and stood up. Bed. Nothing in the world was so important as bed. He squeezed past the desk and had opened the door when he remembered what had niggled his mind: the numbers of the two missing cheques for small amounts had both ended in a 2. A coincidence? But this was a coincidence on top of a discrepancy. He shut the door and went back to the desk. He searched through the bank statements and found a third one on which was recorded a small cheque not paid in: the end number was again 2. He went through the rest of the accounts for the current year and found a fourth missing cheque that ended in 2.

Excitement banished tiredness. These similarities weren't all coincidences, these meant something. There had been two hijackings in the past year and there were four small missing cheques for the same period. Yet how could cheques for such small amounts have any meaning when one was searching for tens of thousands of pounds?

He pushed all the other papers to one side in an untidy heap and put the four statements together. As he studied them, he lit his pipe. He had just blown out the match when he realised that on each statement a cheque for several thousands of pounds had been drawn and these large cheques all ended in a 7.

He began to pace the floor, even though he could only go two paces in each direction: the movement helped him think.

You drew a very small cheque and sent it off and it wasn't paid in . . . You drew a very large cheque and sent it off and it was paid in . . . He stopped pacing and looked at the dates. A cheque for thirty-five shillings had been made out in the second week of July and not paid in: a cheque for

217

three thousand eight hundred-odd pounds
had been put through the bank on July
the fourteenth: a cheque for just over
four thousand eight hundred had been
put through on August the twentieth: a
cheque for two pounds two and six had
been made out on August the sixteenth.

He paced the floor once more. How did
the two sets of cheques tie up? What was
the significance of the fact that the small
cheques all ended in a 2 and the large ones
in a 7?

He brought his own cheque-book out
of his pocket and examined the unused
cheques in it. The numbers were in
computer-style figures and he realised
how easy it would be for a skilled forger
to change a 2 into a 7. That told him
how Sharman had been able to sell the
stolen whisky without any record of the
sales appearing in the accounts.

14

F USIL stood by the side of Kywood's
desk in the latter's office and spread
out the four bank statements. "These
record the small cheques never cashed by
the payees in this year and also the large
cheques which were cashed. The way the
whole thing was worked was this. Two
or three weeks before organising a hi-
jacking, Sharman drew two cheques on
the main account of the parent firm:
one was for a very small amount, one
was for a large amount that came within
the normal monthly order from MacLaren.
The cheques did not correspond to their
stubs. The one ending in a two was made
out to MacLaren, the two at the end of
the number was changed to a seven, and
the forged stamp of MacLaren's bank was
used to make it seem the cheque had been
paid into that bank in the normal way. The
cheque ending in the seven was made out to
a third party for the same amount and was
paid into the third party's bank. When that

was returned to Sharman in the normal course of events by Sharman's bank, he pulled it out and destroyed it. D'you see what we're left with?"

"I think so," replied Kywood doubtfully.

Fusil used four pieces of paper to represent two cheques and their stubs. "The two stub is made out for thirty-five shillings, the two cheque is made out to MacLaren: the two on the cheque is changed into a seven and the stamp of MacLaren's bank is forged. The seven stub is made out to MacLaren and the seven cheque is made out to the third party. Sharman is the third party, of course, and pays the cheque into a cover account at another bank. All that remains now is to forge MacLaren's monthly statement. The amount of whisky corresponding to the cheque drawn is introduced into the warehouse — after the export labels have been soaked off and ordinary ones stuck on — and from then on it's shipped to the shops and sold in the ordinary way. The shops remit the money for the sale to the parent company. In Sharman's books, he has paid out so many thousands of pounds for so many bottles of whisky and the money received from the shops is what is to be expected on the sale of these bottles. This is repeated, which disposes of all the stolen whisky. The bank statements — no longer listing payees since computerisation — are O. K. because all they show are that a few cheques for very small amounts have not been cashed and this is something that often happens. The used cheques match the stubs and the bank statements, the numbers of bottles handled both by the warehouse and the shops agree with the figures of stocks in and out."

Kywood stared at the slips of paper Fusil had used in demonstration. He ran the palm of his hand over his sleek black hair. "The one thing that can't be hidden is the difference between the faked monthly account from MacLaren Distilleries and the true copy in MacLaren's hands."

"Quite, but who's ever going to think of checking one against the other until it's known for certain that Sharman has rigged the books and this was how he did it . . . And all enquiries merely went to show he hadn't rigged a thing."

Kywood fidgeted with his nose. "What's your next move?"

"We've got to have sufficient proof to arrest him before he begins to suspect we're finally on to him. If we don't, he'll either cut and run or destroy all existing evidence. The difference between the monthly statements will show something was up, but legally it won't be enough proof. A good defence counsel could make hash of that."

"Get hold of his books, the used cheques . . . "

"Asking for them will immediately alert him — don't forget we've had them once and cleared them. What we've got to do is discover where he hid the bottles of whisky that weren't immediately introduced into the warehouse and what bank and name he used for the cover account."

Kywood sucked his lips. "That's a hell of a tall order."

"Tall, or not, that's the task."

"You don't think . . . " Kywood became silent.

Fusil did not admit, except to himself, that his real aim and object was to be able to wrap up everything so that he could present Sharman with all the facts in one go and so prove Sharman wasn't the cleverest man in town.

Kerr entered the Westminster Bank in Patton Street and went along to the far counter where he spoke to the cashier. He asked to see the manager.

"I'm sorry," replied the cashier, "he's with a customer and won't be free for a long time. Can the assistant manager help?"

"I'm sure he can."

While he waited, Kerr turned and watched the customer at the nearest counter. He was dressed in clothes that no self-respecting second-hand dealer would deign to touch, but in return for his cheque he was given a bundle of ten-pound notes. He stuffed the notes into the top pocket of his torn and badly stained jacket and slouched out. What racket was he in? wondered Kerr cynically.

The cashier came back and directed Kerr to the office, next door to the manager's room, which was reached directly from the general area. Kerr went into the room. Chambers, a young man full of self-confidence, but not bumptiousness, followed almost immediately. He shook hands, then sat down behind the table.

"How can we help you, Constable?"

"We're searching for an account that was probably opened around two years ago and into which infrequent but pretty big sums of money have been paid. We don't know the name the person will have given, but we can give you a list of the approximate dates and amounts." Kerr took a duplicated list from his coat pocket and passed it across.

Chambers looked quickly through it. "You're presenting us with a bit of a job — still, these are large enough sums to be immediately identifiable. It'll take quite some time, though."

"Can I leave it with you and you ring the station if you have any luck?"

"Sure, I'll do that. What's your telephone number?"

Kerr gave the number, thanked the other, then left. He walked a couple of hundred yards along the street, the main shopping street in Ribstowe, and entered Barclays Bank. The manager proved to be an ill-tempered man who didn't see why any of his staff should waste their precious time merely to assist the police. In reply Kerr, exhibiting a degree of tact that would have astounded many, said how grateful they would be for the help and how it was only the public's assistance that enabled the police to do their job and help keep the country safe for honest people.

Back outside on the pavement, Kerr took a list of banks and their addresses from his pocket. If he met with no success with all the banks in Fortrow, Fusil was going to ask for the county force's co-operation to check on all county banks. It was a job that was going to keep a lot of people employed for a long time.

A clock struck the half hour: half past twelve. He looked along the street and saw a number 92 bus approaching the nearby stop. A 92 went past Helen's office. Even D.C.s, he thought as he ran to the stop, had to eat if they weren't to starve to death.

A green Fortrow Urban District Council van, with canvas body and towing a trailer, was parked in the road a hundred yards down from the entrance to Sharman's warehouse. Rowan, wearing ragged and dirty clothes, slowly swept the rubbish along in the gutter. He'd never before had such a menial job and was quite certain he'd been picked for it because of a personal enmity on the part of either Fusil or Braddon. In the body of the truck, hidden by the canvas, Detective Sergeant Walsh, camera ready on his lap, kept watch through a spy hole. He also hated the job since the day had that kind of raw damp that gradually dug into a man's body.

A van came down the road and turned through the gateway of the warehouse. The driver hooted twice and Sharman came out of the office. He waved at the van driver and walked across the forecourt to unlock the doors of the warehouse.

Walsh took two photographs of Sharman as he unlocked the doors. He took two of the van driver as the latter leaned out to speak to Sharman.

Rowan swept the messy mixture of leaves, dirt, and rotting paper, close to the trailer. He unclipped a shovel, scooped up some of the dirt, and emptied it into the trailer. Careless that the job was only half done, he closed the trailer lid, clipped the shovel back on, went to the rear of the truck and threw the broom inside. "All right?" he demanded.

"Not yet. We've still got to nail the woman."

"To hell with her, Sarge. We can always say she wasn't around."

"You get back to sweeping the gutters. I'll tell you when work stops."

Rowan swore.

Fusil had lunch at the canteen. He arrived late and there was no choice of main dish: it was sausages and mash or go hungry. The sausages had a rind of congealed fat and the mash was lumpy with lumps that looked most unpotato-like. Fusil noticed neither of these facts being almost unaware of what he was eating.

Had he correctly evaluated Sharman's character? Was Sharman so cocky, so sure of himself, that he could not begin to believe himself in danger, even though Stretley, Playford, and Hicks had been picked up by the police? Would the police discover in which bank Sharman had cached the money — it surely had to be a bank because the transfer of money had been by cheque — and where he had stored the stolen whisky until it was time to bring it into the warehouse? The bank

227

surely couldn't be too far away — wouldn't Sharman want to be able to get his hands on the money at short notice at any time?

Once it could be proved that Sharman had organised the hi-jackings and had then sold the whisky through the chain of cut-price liquor shops, was it going to be easy to prove he had murdered Finnigan? All the facts of Finnigan's death surely went to show it was an integral part of the stolen whisky set-up, but no clues had been uncovered definitely to link the two together. No clues had been uncovered that would name Sharman the murderer.

Fusil finished the sausages and mash and pushed the plate to one side. He began to eat the anaemic-looking lemon curd tart.

All the police needed was some luck. Luck to help them uncover the bank account and luck to help them find the place where the whisky had been stored. Then Sharman could be arrested. That would wipe out the bitter memory of his amused contempt and scorn.

He finished the lemon curd tart. Life was so often ironic. Sharman had started his business in order to set up an outlet for stolen whisky: yet the business had flourished so that he could have worked honestly and still made a lot of money, if more slowly. Under different circumstances, Sharman might have ended up a rich elder of the city: another Findren.

Welland walked down the street, checking the numbers of the shops and offices as he went. His mind was very busy — could he join the lads next Saturday evening at the local for a few noisy pints, or would Molly put her foot down and demand he stayed at home? She was only a soft slip of a woman, but she told him what he could do and what he couldn't. He loved her for her bossiness.

He reached number 47 and jerked his mind back to work. On the ground floor of the building were estate agents and on the first and second floors a firm of accountants. There were photographs of houses for sale in the small display window: he was perpetually amazed at the money people could afford to pay for a home. What policeman ever had any hope of saving thousands of pounds? Behind the reception desk of the estate agents was a man of his own age, but half the size and looking as if a fresh south-wester would blow him off his feet. The clerk stopped typing and looked up.

"I'm from the borough police," said Welland. "I gave you a ring earlier on."

"Yes, of course." The clerk seemed to eye Welland with a certain nervous interest. "You wanted to know of any warehouses and lock-up garages we first let about two years ago?"

"That's right."

"I checked through our books and all I could find were the six lock-up garages at the end of Bookers Road. We handle them exclusively."

"Have you been able to draw up a list of renters?"

The clerk went to his desk and brought back a sheet of paper which he pushed across to Welland. "Those are the people who rent 'em now — you see five and six are taken by the same bloke. Except for them, the tenants have changed since two years back. Never had any trouble finding new tenants — and that's even with the rent going up. I'm telling you there's money in lock-up garages." The clerk spoke as if this was an exclusive, red-hot tip.

Numbers five and six were rented by J. Gresham. Welland put the tip of his thick forefinger on the name. "What d'you know about this bloke?"

The clerk shrugged his thin shoulders. "Can't say, really. You'd have to speak to Mr. Brocker for that."

"Right. Let's have a word with him, then."

"I don't know. He's a very busy man."

Mr. Brocker proved not to be too busy to see Welland. He listened quietly, then took out a file from the metal cabinet behind his desk. "The letting was carried out by telephone and letter. The yearly rent is paid in advance."

"Have you met Mr. Gresham?"

"No. As I said, everything's been arranged over the telephone."

"Was there a lease?"

"Only an exchange of letters. It saves money and is all that's necessary for this sort of letting."

"Do you know the name of his firm?"

"Same as his, I suppose. Everything's been done in his name."

"Where d'you send receipts and things?"

Brocker looked at the folder. "Twelve, Madders Road."

"Where's that?"

"I don't know off-hand. I'll check in the street guide." Brocker searched in the index of the guide, looked back at the file, checked the index again and then turned to the indicated map. His expression became perplexed. "It's down by the cemetery at Hanham — bit of a slum. Odd place for a firm. I'd've thought they could find parking nearer."

"You've obviously never checked before?"

"Why should I? The money was paid in advance. In any case, the letting of a lock-up is hardly a very big transaction."

"What about duplicate keys to get into them — do you hold any?"

"Yes, we do. The tenants are always losing theirs and rushing to us for help."

"Can we have a look at numbers five and six, together with the others, if necessary?"

Brocker called in the clerk and gave orders to the clerk to go along with Welland to the garages.

The walk was brief. Throughout it, the clerk eagerly questioned Welland about the case and it was clear that he would be very disappointed if they did not find at least one dead body.

The garages, made from concrete blocks and with asbestos corrugated roofing, stood at the end of a road of semi-detacheds. The up-and-over doors were painted in different colours, to try to mitigate the essential ugliness of the buildings, but it would have taken more than paint to do this. The clerk opened number six, after a short struggle with the lock, and Welland stepped inside. It was empty and the only sign of past occupation was a small oil stain on the floor towards the rear. He walked slowly round the garage. There was nothing to say whether this place had ever been used to store the stolen whisky.

They went into number five. At first sight, the garage was as empty as the first, but as he walked up the right-hand wall, Welland saw an old and oily rag in the corner. He picked it up and examined it and found underneath an inch-square piece of oil-stained brown cardboard. He turned the cardboard over. There were two bits of printing on this side: parts of either the tops or bottoms of the loops of letters. Because of their proximity, these two letters had to be following each other. What were they? b's, f's, g's, h's, k's, i's ... Into his mind came the word 'Highland' — MacLaren's Highland Whisky.

The clerk had been watching his face. "Is that bit of stuff important?"

"It could be," replied Welland.

"Doesn't look it," muttered the other, disappointed by the insignificance of a scrap of oily cardboard.

Welland put the piece of cardboard between two pages of his notebook and held these together with a rubber band. He led the way out of the garage and was about to say he'd finished when he decided he ought, as a matter of form, to check the other four garages — bitter experience had taught him that if he didn't, Fusil would ask if he had.

Numbers four and three were empty and a Morris Traveller was in number two. The clerk was swinging down the door of number two when a Mercedes 220 drew up outside number one and a man in a fur-lined coat and a very sporty check suit climbed out.

"'Afternoon, Mr. Kubick," said the clerk, in deferential tone of voice.

"Hullo, there," replied the other loudly. "How's the world treating you? Have you been picking out all the winners?" He had the air of a man who was pleased to be polite to someone he could really afford to ignore.

"I can't remember when I last had a winner, Mr. Kubick."

"Persevere, my son, persevere, as the bookie said when he took the client's shirt." He stared at Welland. "Having a look at the lock-ups, then?" he asked, in a challenging voice.

The clerk hastened to explain. "This is a detective, Mr. Kubick."

"The law, eh? So what's up? Has someone been a naughty boy round here?" Kubick's manner changed slightly: some of the bombast was replaced by wary watchfulness.

"We're just carrying out general enquiries," said Welland, before the clerk could speak. "Would you know anything about the person or persons who use the last two garages?"

"I wouldn't. What's your interest in 'em?"

Welland ignored the question. "You've never seen them at all?"

"Can't say I have . . . Now that's a lie. I did see one of the end garages used once. As far as I can remember, a van drove out. No idea when it was — long time ago now."

"Would you remember what kind of van it was or whether there were any legends on it?"

"Legends? Like Snow White?"

"A firm's name, that sort of thing," replied Welland, not bothering to smile.

"Heard 'em called lots of things before, but never that." Kubick laughed loudly.

"Do you remember?"

Kubick shrugged his shoulders. "It was just a van."

"Did you see the driver?"

"Gawd knows! I'm telling you, it was a very long time ago."

Welland took from his pocket the three photographs that he'd been given by Braddon immediately after lunch. He handed over the two of Sharman and Sharman's van driver. "Could it have been either of these?"

"Now look, I've just said, it was a long, long time ago. What's more it was night and the bloke inside the van wasn't exactly floodlit. Could've been Frankenstein, for all I know." He again laughed loudly. He was about to hand the photos back when he checked himself. "Here, isn't one of those blokes Sharman?"

"Who?" asked Welland, and for him it was a wonderful display of absolute innocence.

"Jim Sharman. He owns those cut-price liquor stores — made a fortune."

"Don't think I've heard of him," said Welland, as he took the photographs back from the other.

"Well, it certainly looked a bit like him," said Kubick doubtfully. "Pity. It's about time he ended up in jail."

"What makes you say that?"

"I'll tell you. A couple of months ago, I gave him ten to one Caesar's Ghost wouldn't win at Epsom. The old bastard had twenty quid's worth and the bloody horse came in by half the track."

From the look of Kubick, thought Welland, he could lose a lot more money before he went broke.

12, Madders Road was a tobacconist's in

the centre of a row of depressed looking houses: the living-room had many years before been altered into a mean, dingy, kiosk-like shop.

An elderly cripple, with a shock of startlingly white hair, answered Welland's questions. "I got this 'phone call one day, see, asking me to 'old any letters addressed to Gresham and 'e'd collect 'em. Ten quid a year 'e promised."

"What's happened to the letters?"

"There ain't been many in all the time and I've still got 'em. 'E ain't been near for 'em. The ten quid's come regular, though."

"You've never met him?"

"That I ain't."

"How come he telephoned you in the first place and asked you to do this?"

"I ain't no idea, Mister. What's wrong?" His expression was very worried.

Kerr climbed the stairs to the general room and his legs were so tired it seemed they were filled with lead. As he sat down, he sighed with pleasure. It was a piece of unwarranted optimism. The internal telephone on Rowan's desk rang. He stared

238

at it with dislike. If he didn't answer, would it be accepted by the caller that the room was empty? Or would the caller be of a suspicious mind and come along to check? Kerr answered and the caller was Fusil.

"How long have you been back?" demanded Fusil.

"Just stepped inside this moment, sir."

"What about reporting to me?"

"I was on my way in, sir." Kerr replaced the receiver. Heaven was a place in which, should they ever attain it, senior officers were rendered deaf and dumb.

Fusil spoke the moment Kerr entered the room. "Have you had any luck?" It was clear from the unusual eagerness with which he spoke how tensed he was.

"I don't think so, sir. The banks all said they'd check their records and ring here if they uncovered the account we're after. There's no message so I presume no one's discovered it."

Fusil swore. "Have you checked with every bank in town?"

"All except the three in Ascrey Cross. There wasn't time to cover them."

"You'll see them as soon as they open?"

"Yes, sir."

Fusil stared unseeingly at the far wall. "I'll swear the bank he used will be a local one."

There was a heavy knock on the door and Welland entered. He clumped his way over to the desk. "Turned up this, sir, from a lock-up garage in Bookers Road." He opened his notebook, pulled off the rubber band, and dropped the piece of oily cardboard on to the desk.

Fusil picked up the cardboard and studied it.

"I was wondering if those two bits of printing were the tops of an h and an l. You know, MacLaren Highland Whisky," Welland explained carefully, as if Fusil would not otherwise be able to understand.

"Anything else?" asked Fusil.

"I discovered that a bloke called Gresham hired numbers five and six lock-ups and gave twelve, Madders Road as his address. It's a tobacconist and the owner was telephoned way back and offered ten quid a year to hold any letters addressed to Gresham. He's never met Gresham and here are the only letters he ever got."

Welland handed them over.

Fusil opened the letters. They contained receipts and the terms of the agreement. He looked up. "Who'd you see at the estate agents?"

"Mr. Brocker."

Fusil pulled back the cuff of his coat to check on the time by his wrist watch. "Telephone him, explain I must see him and ask if it will be more convenient at his office or home."

Welland left.

Fusil pushed the piece of oily cardboard over to Kerr. "Get on to the county lab and say you're bringing it to them, then rush it up there. Find a comparison cardboard case and take that as well. Tell the lab it's top priority."

Kerr looked doubtful.

Fusil spoke sharply. "What the hell's the matter?"

"The lab always moans that everybody's work is top priority."

"Spin 'em a yarn. You're a good liar."

The Sharmans lived in a large house, set in its own gardens, which they rented for fifteen pounds a week. When they had first moved in, the house had been furnished in the usual negative and characterless fashion of let houses, but Mrs. Sharman had spent a great deal of money on buying expensive furniture to make the place more attractive. She liked furniture which looked as expensive as it was.

They were in the sitting-room, a long, oblong room with a rather ugly fireplace half-way along the outside wall. They were drinking: he had a whisky, she had a gin and tonic. The colour television was on, but neither of them was watching it: she was leafing through a glossy woman's magazine and he was checking some accounts. The telephone rang. "I'll get it," he said. He stood up, finished his drink, and went out into the hall.

"Hullo there, Jim," said the caller breezily. "It's Adrian here. How's the world with you, old boy?"

For a moment, Sharman couldn't identify the other: then he realised it must be Adrian Kubick, a pompous self-opinionated windbag of a man. "'Evening," he said, not bothering to sound pleased.

"I thought you'd be amused by something odd that happened today."

"I'm very busy."

"It won't take a second to tell you. I was driving into my garage — got a new car, don't know if you've seen it? Lovely drop of Mercedes."

"I've too much work . . . "

"Shan't be a second, old boy. Well, I was just opening up the garage when a large bloke comes over and he's a detective. Must say he looked to me more like one of those gorillas you see on the telly playing rugger."

"Go on," said Sharman, all irritated impatience gone.

"The detective asked me about the two end garages and who used 'em. I said I didn't know — only once saw a van coming out of one. 'What did the driver look like?' asked the copper. 'Look, mate,' I said, 'use your loaf. It was dead dark. I couldn't see whether he'd got two noses and three mouths.' " Kubick guffawed. "Then d'you know what he did?"

"I can't guess."

"This'll crease you. He showed me two photos and asked if the driver was either of 'em — and one of the blokes looked exactly like you!"

"Well, I'm damned!" exclaimed Sharman.

"What have you been up to, eh? Swindling the Bank of England?"

"That's right, but not a word to anyone." Sharman was silent for a couple of seconds. "I wonder who it really was?"

"Not knowing, can't say, but I'm telling you, Jim, it was a close relative of yours! Tell you something more. The door in the picture looked like the door of your warehouse."

"Just goes to show the coincidences in life there are, doesn't it?"

"Sure does. I thought you'd be amused."

"Funniest thing I've heard in years. Thanks for calling." Sharman rang off.

He took out his cigar case and chose a cigar. Carefully, he snipped off the end and lit it. The photograph had obviously been taken outside the warehouse at a time when he was completely unaware of what was happening. Further, the police enquiries regarding the lock-up garages meant they had traced where the whisky was hidden each time until he brought it into the warehouse. They had made quite a lot of progress.

It was a shock. He had viewed them

with the same scorn he had always viewed policemen — they were recruited from low intelligence sources and the only reason that any crimes were ever solved was that many criminals were even more unintelligent. Now, purely by luck, these bunglers had cottoned on to him and he was going to have to abandon the business he had built up from nothing. There would be no great financial loss — the shops and warehouse were all on short leases and he never settled accounts with suppliers until the last possible moment so that almost all the liquor in stock was virtually on credit. But nevertheless the loss to him would be very great. He had built up a highly successful business, he had shown all the so-called clever business men of Fortrow that he was a damn sight cleverer than they, and he hated the thought of having to lose his success.

He swore. How could the police really be on to him? True, the detective inspector had appeared to be sharper than normal, but that was hardly saying much. Wasn't the whole thing some sort of coincidence? The police might have been looking around the lock-up garages in connection with a case that had nothing at all to do with the whisky. The photograph could have been of some small-time punk — Kubick was enough of a fool to make that sort of mistake.

Sharman slowly massaged his chin with his left hand. He was, he thought, in danger of deluding himself. He loathed the idea of abandoning the business and therefore was trying to twist the facts to prove to himself there was no need: looked at squarely, the evidence suggested unmistakably that by some perverse stroke of luck, the police were slowly uncovering the truth.

Of course, this didn't begin to add up to failure. Right from the beginning, he'd accepted the fact that things could go wrong from causes beyond his control and he'd naturally planned what to do if this happened. No one could begin to call it a failure when he'd made close on forty thousand from selling the whisky and saved another twenty thousand plus from the business — quite a lot of which was owed to the inland revenue. Even in respect of all this money, he'd proved his cleverness. He'd never left very much in the account, but had bought jewellery

Jewellery was an international currency. Goddamn it, he told himself, the word failure didn't come into it.

He went through to the sitting-room. Judy looked up. She was really beautiful, he thought. The kind of woman other men coveted: the kind of woman to partner a really successful bloke. How many people could even guess that behind her groomed beauty lay a cleverness and toughness of character that almost matched his? Hadn't it been she who'd decided Finnigan had to be killed, when he tried to work out how to avoid murder? Hadn't it been she who'd managed in next to no time to make Finnigan think she was so taken by him that she was panting to climb into the nearest bed with him? She'd handed him the doped whisky and told him that as soon as they'd finished their drinks they'd go for a little walk together — he'd downed his so quickly he'd almost choked. He'd gone out like a light. With Finnigan unconscious, he, Sharman, had come out of hiding and they'd set about getting rid of Finnigan. He'd said they'd sling the unconscious man into the sea with a few lead weights made fast: she'd suggested leaving him in the cellar of the wine shop and setting fire to the place — why not cut down on the competition at the same time as eliminating Finnigan? She'd got brains, no mistake there.

She studied his face. "What's happened, Jim? Something's wrong, isn't it?"

"That was Adrian Kubick. I didn't know it, but he garages his car in Bookers Road. He was driving into his lock-up when a split came up and questioned him and showed him a photo of me taken outside the warehouse. Kubick had seen the van leaving the lock-up and the split wanted Kubick to identify the driver. It means we're blown."

She shrugged her shoulders. "There was always the chance."

He crossed to his chair, picked up the glass, and refilled it. He admired the casual way in which she accepted the news.

"What are we going to do?" she asked.

"Clear out from here. Go down to the office and burn all the papers, then find a hotel for the night. Tomorrow morning we'll draw out what's left in the bank . . . "

"Don't you think it would be better to

248

leave that?" she suggested.

"Hell, no! There's only a thousand or so in the account but we might as well take it with us."

"You don't think the police might be on to that as well?"

"Them? Not those stupid bastards." He laughed harshly. "They must have had a whole goddamn basinful of luck to get as far as they have, but they'll never be able to work out the details."

She looked doubtful, but did not argue further.

15

BROCKER yawned, hoping his visitor would take the hint. Fusil was not the man to do that. "If you could only remember what bank the cheques you received were drawn on?" said Fusil.

"I've already told you, I can't." Brocker wondered what his wife, who was in the kitchen, was thinking? If he was five minutes late for a meal she raised all hell: he hated to think how late he was by now.

"Can you say what colour they were?"

"Inspector," he said plaintively, "I don't remember anything about them. I probably never ever saw them: the handling of cheques isn't my department."

Mrs. Brocker opened the door very noisily. She stared at Fusil with a militant expression. She had a severe face that suggested a character who knew exactly what was right and proper in all things. When she saw that Fusil was not going to be as easily moved as she'd hoped, she left and slammed the door shut.

"Inspector, I'm very sorry but I must . . . " began Brocker, in some desperation.

Fusil interrupted him. "This is absolutely vital. Try to remember at least something that could be of help."

"But I can't."

Fusil sighed.

"It was just a small letting," muttered Brocker. "And it all went smoothly. The money was always paid right on the day, the cheques were always cleared without trouble."

"And you never stopped to wonder why a man should rent two garages for his company and then scarcely ever use them?"

"But how was I to know they weren't being used?"

In the forensic laboratory at H.Q., an assistant used a razor-blade knife to cut a marked section out of the top of the cardboard case that had contained MacLaren whisky. The section exactly matched in size and shape the one found in the lock-up garage.

He put the two pieces of cardboard side-by-side under an adjustable overhead light.

A casual visual examination suggested that the printing was exactly similar.

He used a finely adjustable and slightly modified double-pointed compass to measure the inside and outside thickness of the loops at several different places: the thickness varied very slightly on the control section and these variations were repeated on the crime section. He examined each in turn under a low-power microscope and found a fault in the printing duplicated.

He telephoned Fortrow eastern division H.Q. and spoke to the duty inspector. He said he'd been asked for an interim report as soon as possible: as far as he could tell, there was little doubt the crime section of cardboard had come from the lid of a case of MacLaren whisky, but before he could be positive he needed to carry out long and laborious tests to determine the consistency of the two sections for final comparison. The duty inspector thanked him and said he'd pass on the message immediately to the C.I.D.

Kerr arrived at Helen's house and the door was opened by Mr. Barley.

"Hullo then, John. We'd given you up for lost."

"I was ordered up to Barstone at the last moment, Mr. Barley."

"They're working you, aren't they?"

"There's no rest for the wicked." Kerr stepped inside and shut the door. "You know how things go — the boss-man has to do everything to make certain it's done right." He grinned.

"Then you could maybe do with a quick drink to revive you?" Mr. Barley, gnome-like in appearance, stared up at him and winked.

"That's the best suggestion I've heard today. My throat's like sand-paper. Isn't Helen around?"

"She went upstairs to wash her hair, seeing as you didn't turn up, but no doubt she'll be down quick now." Mr. Barley half turned towards the stairs. "Helen," he shouted, "there's a bloke says he's come to see you."

"D'you mean John?"

"That's right."

"Tell him I can't come for the moment. I've hardly any clothes on."

As far as Kerr was concerned, he'd no

253

objection to her coming down as she was: the thought of her in filmy underclothes was enough to dry out his mouth. The last few weeks had taught him that she was far more passionate, when she wished to be, than previously he would ever have imagined possible. He had agreed with her that they should reserve the full act of making love until they were married, but he hoped the marriage wasn't all that far away.

He followed Mr. Barley into the sitting-room. Mrs. Barley was knitting him a jumper and she asked him to stand so she could measure it against him. When she did so, she muttered in annoyance as it was clear that something had gone wrong across the chest. "Dear me! Are you sure you're the same as last time?"

Mr. Barley laughed as he began to pour out the drinks. "What d'you think he's done, Mother, grown in the night?"

"But I'm sure I checked most carefully. Oh, well, I'll just have to unpick it back to here."

Mr. Barley held up the bottle of MacLaren whisky. "We've all but hammered this, John. I suppose no one's handed out any more free samples?"

"No such luck," Kerr replied. "I've been tramping from bank to bank and not one of 'em's given me so much as a tenner." He sat down, after offering cigarettes. He raised his glass. "Cheers. The first today and all the more welcome."

"Cheers, John." Mr. Barley returned to his chair. "We went up to the transport exhibition today. They'd five steam engines there: real beauties."

Kerr half listened to what was said: this engine had been spotless, that one had needed a polish, this one had represented a revolutionary advance in its day, that one had held some sort of record from London to Newcastle.

Ten minutes later, Helen came into the room, her hair dampened down and her face red from the heat and the rubbing. She sat down on the arm of Kerr's chair. "I didn't think you were going to be able to get here tonight, darling. Have you eaten anything?"

"I haven't, no."

"I'll cook you some sausages and bacon."

"That would be lovely." He sipped the whisky. Just think, once he was married there'd be no more canteen suppers.

Sharman woke up. He brought his left hand from under the bedclothes and checked on the time. Seven minutes to seven. They'd breakfast as close to eight as possible, leave the hotel in a taxi, drive to the bank and withdraw the odd thousand pounds remaining, go down to the docks and catch the next cross-Channel boat. He'd naturally got false passports and so there'd be no hope of tracing them — even if the police did stumble on to sufficient evidence to try to arrest them.

He climbed out of bed and crossed to the chair on which was Judy's pigskin suitcase. He opened it and brought out the jewel case, the key to which was in her handbag. He unlocked the case. Inside was a rope of matched and graded bell pearls, three diamond rings, one ruby coloured, the other two rose pink, and a Mandalay dark red ruby pendant. They were really beautiful and valuable pieces of jewellery.

She spoke suddenly. "What's the matter? Worried someone's nicked 'em in the night?"

He turned and looked at her in bed. "I

didn't know you were awake, love. Just checking." He held the ruby pendant in the palm of his hand. "You won't like selling 'em, will you?"

"I won't, but as soon as you're established again, you can buy me some more."

She had complete faith in him, he thought. She knew he'd make a success of whatever he did — and with her help, he would. By God! she was a real wife. He replaced the pendant, crossed to the bed, and kissed her.

"Steady on, Jim," she murmured, after a while. "We're in a hurry."

"You're dead right there," he answered hoarsely, as he pulled back the bedclothes.

Fusil looked through the window in his office and stared up at the leaden sky which promised rain. He lit his pipe. He longed to be doing something active, yet at the moment he could do nothing but wait.

The telephone rang. He hurried to the desk and answered the call. The desk sergeant reported there was a woman below who was complaining her neighbour was always exhibiting himself and what was she to do? Fusil swore and suggested she had a cold bath.

He returned to the window. Just how vital was time? Sharman believed himself so very clever that no stupid hick of a policeman could ever successfully challenge him: but because he undoubtedly was a clever man, wouldn't he have realised that no plan could ever be a hundred per cent foolproof and therefore it was common sense to make arrangements for a sudden disappearance if circumstances ever warranted it? Did the men out on the case realise the absolute need for discretion?

He looked at his watch. Half past ten. By now, Kerr should have visited all three banks in Ascrey Cross. Suppose the account he was searching for did not turn up in either Fortrow or the county? Should he ask London to make enquiries? If there was no account locally, wasn't it probably because all his theories were wrong? Sharman would surely want any money very close to hand.

The telephone rang again and this time it was Kerr. The National Westminster in Ascrey Cross had no account that could be Sharman's: the other two would be telephoning in as soon as possible. Fusil ordered him over to the estate agents to interview the staff to try to find someone who'd a better memory — and more intelligence — than Brocker.

Fusil replaced the receiver. Almost immediately, there was another call for him from Barclays Bank in Ascrey Cross. He identified himself.

"One of your constables, Inspector, came into this bank earlier on and made some enquiries. D'you know what I'm talking about?"

Fusil silently swore. Did the old fool think he was completely out of touch with what went on in the division? "Yes, I know."

"Well, he asked us to see if we'd an account . . . "

"I told him what he was to ask you. What's the result?"

"That's what I'm trying to tell you, Inspector."

Fusil stared resentfully at the far wall. When time might be more precious than diamonds, this man had to waffle on and on.

"Are you still there?" asked the caller.

"I'm still here," replied Fusil heavily.

"You didn't speak so I wasn't certain if you'd gone away. I've checked up as the young detective asked and have found an account in the name of Mr. Gresham into which fairly large sums were paid at around the dates given. There was one payment in for each date and the sums are roughly equal to the sums your detective gave me, although there are differences . . . "

"What is the greatest difference?"

"Eighty-one pounds, three shillings and sixpence. That seems to me . . . "

"The sum's too small to be of any significance," interrupted Fusil.

"I wasn't certain. As the sums don't exactly match those your detective . . . "

"What's in the account now?"

"Nothing."

"What?" snapped Fusil.

"Soon after each cheque was paid in, most of the money was withdrawn and there was only just over a thousand pounds in the account this morning when Mr. Gresham came in and withdrew everything and . . . "

"When was he in?"

"I'm not certain of the exact time . . . "

"Good God! man, I'm not asking for the nearest second. Roughly when?"

"It was very shortly after the bank opened. In fact, he was probably the first customer."

Fusil swore aloud and there was a shocked exclamation from the man at the other end. "Who paid out the money?" asked Fusil.

"I can't really say."

"Then go and find out who did pay him and get the bloke to the 'phone."

"But I fail to understand . . ."

"Never mind what you don't understand, get hold of the bloke."

Fusil swore again as he waited. They'd missed Sharman by minutes. Why the hell hadn't Kerr started at Ascrey Cross instead of finishing there? It was getting on for ten to eleven. Sharman had something like fifty minutes' start.

"Hullo," said a man who sounded younger and much more alive than the last speaker.

"I gather you paid out to Gresham the money remaining in his account," snapped Fusil. "Will you describe him."

"Well, I'm not very good at that sort of thing, but I'll try. He was quite big: you

261

know, solid, not fat and paunchy. He'd a round, cheerful face and a square sort of a chin: the kind of bloke you look at and instinctively decide is important. He chatted away and seemed quite pleasant — there was only one thing . . . " He became silent.

"Well?"

"It's nothing definite, like — probably it sounds stupid — but I remember catching him looking straight at me and I suddenly thought he was jeering at me. I know that sounds a bit . . . well, a bit daft . . . "

"There's nothing daft about that: you've helped me a treat. Hang on at the bank, will you, and don't move from it until one of my officers brings in a photo for you to look at. Many thanks."

Fusil replaced the receiver on its cradle. The man had been Sharman — there was no room for doubt now. So the fox had bolted. Why? What had alarmed him? Bolted where? North, south, east or west?

Sharman was clever. He'd have summed up all the possibilities. He'd work on the principle that the police were close behind him because that way he'd nothing to lose from over-confidence. A really large city such as London, offered a good hiding place despite all the dangerous publicity there might be if his photograph appeared on television and in the newspapers, because its vastness assured anonymity to the careful person. Yet to a man with money, the Continent perhaps offered the best long-term hiding place. Sharman had been withdrawing the money from the account soon after depositing it and that surely suggested he'd been buying readily cashable securities? This would fit in with the Continental hideout, because money in quantity took up space and on account of the currency regulations the officials at airports and ports were on the watch for the illegal export of money. Jewellery was by far the best bet. Mrs. Sharman could travel with her 'personal' jewellery and this would be sold as and when money was wanted.

If they were making for the Continent, they could go by boat, Hovercraft, or plane. More people travelled together at one time by boat than by either of the other services and a large number of passengers meant a less careful surveillance from Customs and Home Office officials.

A really clever man with strong nerves could work out the probabilities as they would occur to a police officer and then do the least likely, in the equivalent of a double-bluff . . . In other words, hide-up in London. There were many ways and means of minimising the dangers of being identified.

If traffic blocks were set up right now on the two main roads into London, there would still be time to catch him as he wouldn't arrive at the outskirts of London for at least another half hour. If he was going by sea, was there still time? Fusil crossed to one of the filing cabinets and brought out of it the latest cross-Channel time-table. After a frustrating search that had him swearing aloud as he tried to discover the meaning of certain symbols, he found the next sailing was to Calais at eleven o'clock. The passengers would all have boarded.

He stared at the opened time-table. The situation was quite clear. There was not the time, nor were the forces immediately available, thoroughly to cope with both sea and road travel — let alone all the other methods he had mentally discarded. So he had to decide which method of travel Sharman would be using.

Forcing himself to move slowly, he tapped out the ash from his pipe, then filled the bowl with tobacco. Whatever decision he took would be final.

Exactly how clever was Sharman? That was the sixty-four-thousand-dollar question. Fusil recalled how obviously self-satisfied Sharman had been and that decided him: a man who was really clever from beginning to end could never have been so self-satisfied. Sharman would not be carrying out the double-bluff.

Sharman stood by the square porthole. Noise was all around: on the dock men were shouting, electric cranes were working with their peculiar twanging, grinding sounds, and fork-lift trucks' warning bells were clanging, on board there was the muffled tramp of feet from the deck above, while in the cabin the steady hiss of the fresh air ventilating system accompanied the thumping and rhythmical vibration that came from deck and bulkheads.

He looked at his watch and turned. "We're five minutes late sailing."

She didn't answer. She was a very bad sea traveller and was lying down on the lower bunk. She had taken two anti-seasick pills and was praying they would work.

He crossed to the single chair and sat down. It was ridiculous to feel nervous at this point, but he couldn't hide from himself that he did. He lit a cigar. Why in the hell was he still worrying? Nothing could go wrong now.

From outside there came some shouting. He heard a distant jangle of bells and the rhythm of the thumping vibration changed. He stood up and looked through the porthole again and was in time to see the crane slide out of view to the right. They were under way.

"Is the sea rough?" she asked.

"As smooth as a pond," he said, although he'd no idea because it would be some time before they steamed out of the river into the sea.

They swung in the centre of the dredged channel and then steamed downstream. As they passed the Old Docks, Sharman stared at the jumble of cranes, sheds, and ships: somewhere beyond them, the police were still scratching around, trying to find the proof that he'd organised the stealing and selling of the whisky and had murdered Finnigan. Unless they were even luckier than they had been, they wouldn't find the proof: if, by some miracle, they did, he wouldn't be around for the discovery to do them any good.

He blew out a cloud of fragrant cigar smoke. He found it odd, now, to reflect on the fact that they'd murdered Finnigan. The episode had for him the same vague unreality of a dream half-remembered: perhaps that was because everything had been so peaceful. Finnigan had been snoring when they left him in the cellar, totally unconscious of the fact that his life had little time to run. A dream-like memory, thought Sharman, but one that gave pleasure. One of the German philosophers had pin-pointed the foundation of such pleasure. When a man destroyed another human, he was usurping God.

They passed the shallows, then Tawsey Head, and the boat began to move to the long, but shallow, swell. The bulkheads creaked gently.

"It's rough," she moaned. She retched

twice. "You told me it was calm. But it's rough."

He was sorry for her, but also comforted that she possessed this weakness — he never felt seasick. He rang the bell for a steward and when one knocked and entered, he ordered a bottle of Heidsieck, Dry Monopole.

The champagne came in a tarnished ice-bucket with only a few pieces of ice in it. Sharman complained about the lack of ice, but the steward was sullenly uninterested and merely demanded the money.

After the steward had gone, Sharman offered his wife some champagne. She moaned, rolled over in the bunk, and faced the bulkhead. He filled his glass, raised it in a salute to his success, and sipped the champagne. There was a knock on the door. "Come in," he said.

Fusil, followed by Kerr, entered. "You're still doing yourself well, then," said Fusil and he didn't try to hide his malicious pleasure.

Sharman sat on the far side of the table in the interview room. His blue eyes now reflected only harsh, animal cunning.

"Why were you going abroad?" asked Fusil.

"For a holiday, why else?"

"Why travel on false passports?"

"I obtained the passports to win a bet that you could always buy false ones if you wanted. I decided to use them on this trip to find out if anyone would ever suspect they were false."

"You can hardly expect me to believe that load of nonsense."

"Prove it's a lie."

Kerr, sitting to the right of the door and taking notes, looked quickly up at Fusil's face. The D.I. was trying hard to keep his expression neutral, but was failing to conceal his growing frustration and anger.

Sharman took out his cigar case and helped himself to the last cigar. Somehow, he managed to make the ritual of cutting the end, striking the match and waiting for the flame to clear, and the lighting of the cigar, a declaration that he was far too big and clever ever to be seriously worried by a mere detective inspector on a small provincial force.

"Why go on acting the fool?" asked Fusil. "You know we've got you for the theft and selling of the whisky and the murder of Finnigan."

"My dear inspector," said Sharman, "whatever are you talking about?"

"You made contact with the chief steward on the *Maltechara* and bribed him to tell you when a load of whisky was due. You paid Stretley to hi-jack the lorry. When the lorry was left at the pre-arranged spot, you unloaded the whisky into another vehicle and drove off with it. You introduced roughly half of each load into your warehouse immediately — after you'd changed the labels — and the other half you stored in the two lockup garages in Bookers Road.

"Everything worked smoothly until the hi-jacking at the end of July. Finnigan decided to put the black on you and stayed behind to keep watch on the lorry. He surprised you and tried to blackmail you. To ensure your safety, you murdered him by drugging him and leaving him in the cellar of Verlay's Wine Store, which you fired."

"I admire your imagination, if nothing else," said Sharman, in mocking tones. "Tell me, the chief steward of the ship you've just named — has he tried to say he identifies me?"

"He has identified you."

Sharman smiled.

Fusil took out his pipe and began to scrape the bowl with the small blade of a penknife.

"And do the men you claim carried out the hi-jacking identify me?" asked Sharman.

"Yes," snapped Fusil.

"As I've never met them in my life, this must take some doing."

"Wriggle all you like, we've got you," said Fusil roughly. "We can prove the route of the stolen whisky through your warehouse and the shops, we can prove Finnigan was in on the hi-jacking, we can . . . "

Sharman used his cigar as a pointer to underline his words. "I'm quite certain you'll be able to prove nothing. It's all lies."

"Your books will give us plenty of proof."

"D'you mean my accounts which you recently had checked and which were cleared?"

"At the time, we didn't compare your monthly statements from MacLaren with their copies held by them."

Sharman puffed at the cigar. He blew out the smoke in a fine jet. "It's bad luck for you, but I happened to burn all the papers you're talking about as they were cluttering up the office."

Fusil spoke with heavy sarcasm. "No jury is going to miss the significance of that timing."

"What significance is there in burning papers and old cheques which my accountants had seen and the police had examined and cleared?"

"MacLaren's accounts will show the gaps when you didn't buy any whisky from them — yet you kept on selling it in the shops. If you were honest, how come you were able to buy all the jewellery in your wife's possession?"

"Have you overlooked the possibility that it was left to my wife by her aunt?"

"Give me the aunt's name and the date of her death." Fusil waited, then said: "To save you the trouble of thinking up any further lies, I'll tell you how we work. We know the dates you drew money out o.

Barclays Bank in Ascrey Cross and we have the pieces of jewellery which are obviously good ones and therefore easily identifiable. Only jewellers in pretty big towns would sell jewellery of such quality. It won't take very many enquiries to discover which jewellers sold the pieces and the dates of the sales. When the dates and the amounts are shown to coincide near enough with the amounts and dates of withdrawals from the bank, the set-up becomes obvious."

When Sharman next spoke, he seemed a shade less confident. "The jewellery was bought with loans from the company."

"The loans didn't appear in the accounts."

"I . . . I made certain they didn't."

"How?"

Sharman did not answer.

"How is it that the value of the stolen whisky corresponds with the two amounts paid into your bank each time?"

Sharman tapped the ash from his cigar with a gesture that betrayed nervousness.

"We've got you," said Fusil, "tight and square."

"You can't prove anything. You haven't any right to hold me now. I demand to see my solicitor."

"You're guilty of travelling on forged passports."

"I've explained what happened."

"You're also guilty of attempting to smuggle currency out of the country."

"No."

"You withdrew just over a thousand quid from the bank this morning."

"I gave that money to a friend."

Fusil smiled wolfishly, his self-confidence fully restored. "Shall we rip your luggage apart and if we don't find it start on your clothes? Do you particularly want to be subjected to the degradation of a close physical search? Wouldn't you prefer to be sensible and tell me where you've hidden the money?"

Sharman stubbed out his cigar in the ash-tray.

Fusil said: "You can start stripping while I give orders for your luggage to be searched."

"The money's sewn into my coat," Sharman muttered.

Mrs. Sharman was both sullen and scornful. "Don't be so soft," she said.

Fusil studied her and wondered just

who had provided the motivating force for their crimes. "I'm sorry you don't like the news, but your husband has made a full confession."

"Give over."

"He's admitted organising the hi-jacking, storing part of the whisky in the garages in Bookers Road, altering the numbers on the cheques, faking MacLaren's monthly statements, banking the money in Ascrey Cross, buying your jewellery with this money, and killing Finnigan because he tried to put the black on both of you."

"Your name ought to be Hans Bloody Christian Andersen."

No one could call her the weaker sex, thought Fusil.

Kywood arrived at Sharman's house just as the search was being concluded on Wednesday afternoon. He spoke to a P.C. who went upstairs and told Fusil the D.C.I. had arrived. Fusil, reluctantly, went downstairs.

"Have you found much?" asked Kywood.

"We've found nothing," Fusil replied heavily.

Kywood chewed his lower lip for a

few seconds. "Aren't there any traces of barbiturates about the place?"

"No, none."

"What about candles to give a comparison with the burnt wick?"

"Not a candle in the place."

"Do they keep paraffin here?"

"No."

"Goddamn it!" muttered Kywood. He was silent for a short while, then said: "Well, Bob, how's it looking?"

"Not as bright as it could be," admitted Fusil, "but we've still got a very respectable case."

"Have we?"

"Of course."

"But as I understand it, they've admitted nothing and have burned all the papers. Doesn't that leave us out on a limb? We make allegations about how the whisky was sold, they deny them. We can't prove beyond all doubt that we're right — especially when we checked and cleared all their books earlier on."

Bitterly, Fusil remembered how Kywood had been so certain that the investigations into Sharman and Findren's businesses were totally unnecessary that he had drastically restricted the time available to Inspector Melchett. If he hadn't implanted his disbelief into Melchett's mind, if Melchett had had more time, might not the fraud have been uncovered then — when all the proof of it was to hand?

"Well?" demanded Kywood.

"They can't wriggle round the dates and amounts of money paid into the bank in Ascrey Cross under a false name."

"You know as well as me that that sort of evidence doesn't stand up when a good criminal lawyer starts playing around with it." Kywood shook his head. "I'm telling you, Bob, unless you can find some definite evidence — good, physical evidence the jury can look at and understand — it's going to be tricky going." His voice gained a note of petulance. "I told you you ought to have gone to Sharman's office and grabbed all the firm's books the moment we were certain, but you were too stubborn."

Kywood, thought Fusil bitterly, had the very useful faculty of always being able to prove that it was the other bloke who was wrong.

16

KERR arrived at Helen's house at a quarter to seven that evening. She kissed him on the cheek, then stepped back. "You look really tired, darling."

"I am. But I'm also tough!" He grinned at her. "I'll survive."

In the sitting-room, Mrs. Barley said: "Good Heavens, John, whatever's the matter? You look completely worn out."

"I am pretty tired, Mrs. Barley. We've been at it hard all day."

"You mustn't let them make you do so much," said Helen, a note of asperity in her voice.

He smiled. "You've met my boss — he's not the kind of man you argue with. He works himself until he's ready to drop and expects everyone else to do the same."

"I don't care what he expects."

Mr. Barley chuckled. "Come on, you two women, stop clucking. John's all right. Hard work never killed anyone."

278

"I'll thank you to mind your own business," said Mrs. Barley.

Mr. Barley winked at Kerr. "Like an old hen."

"You'd be the first to complain if I didn't fuss over you," she said. She spoke to Kerr. "Sit down, John, and get warmed up: it's a cold night. Here, Father, get out of that chair and let John have a warm."

"Never allowed a moment's peace, I'm not," complained Mr. Barley, with mock indignation as he moved to the settee.

Kerr sat down and warmed his hands before the blazing coal fire. Helen stood by the arm-chair. "Can I get you something, John? How about some tea?"

"Tea!" exclaimed Mr. Barley scornfully. "D'you think a man who's all clapped out from work wants a cup of tea — I'm telling you, he wants something a good bit stronger than that."

"Then why don't you give it to him," said Mrs. Barley, "instead of just talking about it?"

Mr Barley stood up. "There's a wee drop of whisky left or plenty of beer."

"The beer will do fine . . . " began Kerr.

"You'll have the whisky," said Mrs. Barley, "because it'll do you a world more good."

"Mother, if he really prefers beer . . ." began Helen.

"He really prefers the whisky," replied Mrs. Barley.

Kerr did not argue. There were times when Mrs. Barley could become a little bossy, but on this occasion she was quite right and it had only been politeness which had prompted him to ask for beer.

Mr. Barley left the room, returning shortly with the bottle of MacLaren whisky, two cans of beer, four glasses, and a jug of water. He and Helen had beer, his wife and Kerr had whisky. "There's a dead man," he said, as he put the bottle of whisky back on the tray.

"It's your birthday soon, love," said Mrs. Barley. "Maybe I'll save a bit and buy you another bottle as your present."

"It's not worth it when the government makes it cost so much," he protested though without much force. He sat down and raised his glass. "Here's good health to everyone."

They drank.

"What's so special about today to wear you right out?" asked Helen.

"I told you we arrested the Sharmans yesterday on the boat and brought them back here — we've been going hammer and tongs all today trying to tie up loose ends."

"What kind of loose ends?" asked Mr. Barley.

"In a case like this, there's always trouble over proof. You know, the courts demand absolute proof of everything the prosecution alleges. Well, it's not always easy. Take this case. We know what the truth is, but finding the proof of it . . . " He became silent, suddenly realising how garrulous he was becoming over a case that was not yet closed.

"And you're not having much luck?" asked Mr. Barley, showing the usual eagerness with which he followed Kerr's cases.

"Things are a bit tricky," he answered, with deliberate vagueness. He stared at a piece of burning coal which was giving off a blue flame. If, in any trial, the prosecution's case was shown up by the defence to be weak on an important part, the jury's sympathy swung round to the defence and they were inclined to seek an even higher degree of proof of the accused's guilt than before. A good defence counsel would very soon pick holes in this case.

Where the hell was the proof that was needed to nail the Sharmans once and for all? Surely they couldn't be as clever as they believed themselves. Fusil must crack the case. He was a real sharp, clever bastard and Sharman wasn't in the same league.

Mrs. Barley stood up. "I'll go and get supper. Helen, you can come and give me a hand."

Helen drained her glass. "Coming, Mother," she said dutifully. She rested her hand on Kerr's shoulder in a gesture of warn intimacy, then followed her mother out of the room.

Mr. Barley began to talk enthusiastically about a friend of his who had spent the last six years building a model steam locomotive. Kerr allowed his mind to wander as he stared once more at the fire. Nobody was smarter than Fusil, certainly not a round-faced, smooth haired bloke with jeering blue eyes . . . "Good God!" he exclaimed suddenly.

"I don't know that it's all that unusual," said Mr. Barley. "After all, a lot of people make models . . . "

"The whisky bottle." Kerr jumped to his feet.

"Here, what's up?" cried a thoroughly startled Mr. Barley.

Kerr didn't bother to answer, but ran out of the room, across the hall, and into the kitchen. Mrs. Barley was by the stove and Helen was using a fork to work at something in a basin.

"Where's that bottle of whisky you brought out on the tray?" he asked excitedly.

"What on earth?" said Mrs. Barley, flustered by his manner.

"Have you thrown it out?"

"Of course I have since it was empty."

"Where's the dustbin?"

"Outside, where it always is. But what d'you . . . " She stopped as he flung open the door and went out to the small paved area beyond.

He unclipped the lid of the plastic dustbin and picked up the bottle which was lying on top of the rubbish. Was Sharman's gesture of contemptuous generosity going to fix him?

Kerr telephoned Fusil's house from the nearest call-box. He spoke to Mrs. Fusil who said her husband was still at the station. Kerr searched his pockets for another sixpence, found two, and called the police station. The duty sergeant said the D.I. had left an hour ago and he'd no idea where he was. No new crime had been reported.

Kerr left the call-box and stood on the pavement in the fine drizzle that had started to fall. Fusil hadn't suddenly been called out to a new crime, so why wasn't he at home? Ten to one, because he was a man who didn't know how to admit defeat, he was out at Sharman's house, doggedly trying to uncover evidence of some significance.

Members of the C.I.D. were only allowed to claim taxi expenses in emergencies. This, Kerr decided, was an emergency. He used his last sixpence to telephone for a taxi.

The taxi drove him quickly across town to Sharman's house, in the drive of which was parked the D.I.'s battered Vauxhall. Kerr paid the taxi, adding a tip which he considered very generous but the driver plainly didn't, and then walked up to the front door. It was locked and he rang the bell.

Fusil was plainly surprised to see him. "What are you doing here?" he asked abruptly.

"I've brought this bottle." Kerr held it up.

"I can see that," replied Fusil, his voice a shade colder.

"It's the one Sharman gave me at the warehouse."

Fusil's expression changed.

"D'you remember you asked to see inside one of the cases. He picked out a bottle and offered it to you and when you refused he threw it across to me. I'll bet a fortune this is one of the stolen bottles and he was laughing himself sick because he was giving it to me and I was too dumb to know. If I'm right, the label's been changed — he or his wife must have done the changing and a set of dabs could just be on the inside. I doubt he'd have been clever enough to think of that."

"No," said Fusil, "I doubt he would. Can you prove it's the same bottle he gave you?"

"I passed it on to my future father-in-law the same day that we went to the warehouse."

"And he's only just finished it now?"

"Yes. He gave me and Mrs. Barley the last two tots tonight."

"You've got a wonderful future father-in-law," said Fusil. "Shove it in the back of my car. And handle it as if it were more precious than diamonds. When you've done that, come back in here."

"I'd better get back to the house, sir. Supper was being cooked . . ."

"Haven't you yet learned to stop thinking about your goddamn stomach?"

Kerr, feeling mutinous, took the bottle out to the Vauxhall. When he returned to the hall, he found Fusil had not moved.

"I came back here," said Fusil slowly, "trying to work out if there was anything more I could do. This place has been searched and nothing found, but you've just reminded me that Sharman wasn't all that clever, after all. He's maybe made other mistakes that haven't yet been uncovered. You and I can carry out a second search and we'll make certain we don't leave a single piece of dust unturned."

"Couldn't you have a quick look for barbiturates . . . " began Kerr.

"We have."

"Then perhaps if we found a candle we could send it to the lab tomorrow . . . "

"I'm not a goddamn idiot," snapped Fusil. "I've covered all the obvious points."

"Then don't you think, sir, that it would be better to leave the search until daylight . . . "

"No."

Dismally, Kerr remembered how close he had been to eating supper.

The search was utterly methodical and thorough and by the time they had finished the last of the five bedrooms, Kerr was so tired that he could think of nothing but bed — that was, until his stomach gurgled twice and he realised he could never sleep until he had eaten. Mrs. Barley was a first-class cook. Had she been preparing for supper one of her superb steak and kidney puddings with a gravy so rich that it was almost a meal in itself?

"We'd better move, I suppose," said Fusil despondently.

"Yes, sir," said Kerr enthusiastically.

"But, goddamn it, there must be something here."

"There can't be," said Kerr hastily. "We've been over everything everywhere."

Fusil hesitated, then led the way out of the room, down the stairs, and across the hall to the front door. He switched off the hall light and closed and locked the front door behind him.

The drizzle had increased and turned into rain. It was one of those nights when even a duck would have felt dismal.

"I was wondering . . . " began Kerr, then stopped.

"What?" asked Fusil, as he switched on a torch.

"I was wondering if you were going anywhere near Prior Lane on your way home, sir?"

"What is it — d'you want a lift?"

"If there's one going."

"All right. When we've finished."

"Finished?" cried Kerr dismally.

"You don't think we're leaving until we've searched the garage, do you?"

Kerr's stomach, as if in dire protest gurgled again.

Fusil unlocked the garage, stepped inside

and switched on the light. It was of large double size, nearly twenty feet square. Against the far wall was a work bench.

"You take that side," ordered Fusil. "I'll take this one. And check all the dirt and muck, don't just look at it."

Kerr slowly moved along the right-hand wall. He found a length of wood with which to search the considerable quantity of oily and greasy rubbish that littered the floor and work bench, but even so some of the muck got on to his hands. What a life! Half past ten at night and he was poking around in filth.

"By God!" shouted Fusil suddenly, his voice high with excitement. "Come on over here and have a look at this."

Kerr hurried across the floor. Fusil had brushed off some dust that had lain on top of a thin layer of greasy dirt. The dirt had formed a mould and in it was a circular impression which had one segment cut off: along the straight line was a V-shaped mark. Kerr instantly recalled the base of the hydraulic jack that had been used to force open the steel bars of the cellar in which Finnigan had been burned to death.

"We've got him," said Fusil triumphantly.

Fusil dropped Kerr outside Helen's house and drove off. Kerr stood on the pavement and stared up and saw all the rooms were in darkness. Dismally, he turned and was about to begin the long walk home — all buses having stopped by now — when the hall light was switched on. He went up to the front door and knocked.

"Who's that?" Helen called out.

"It's me — John."

She opened the door and he went in. "I thought I heard a car," she said.

She was wearing a dressing gown over a flowered nightdress, which peeped demurely from underneath. "Mummy and Daddy have gone to bed, but Mummy said you were bound to come back for a meal. She's left it warming in the oven for you."

"She's wonderful," he said enthusiastically. "What's on the menu? Her very special steak and kidney pie with all that lovely thick gravy?"

She laughed. "Good Heavens, no. Nothing like that tonight. Four fish-cakes and some mashed potato."

He put his arm round her and felt the swell of her breast. A man couldn't have everything, he thought philosophically.

THE END

NURSE ALICE IN LOVE
Theresa Charles

Accepting the post of nurse to little Fernie Sherrod, Alice Everton could not guess at the romance, suspense and danger which lay ahead at the Sherrod's isolated estate.

POIROT INVESTIGATES
Agatha Christie

Two things bind these eleven stories together — the brilliance and uncanny skill of the diminutive Belgian detective, and the stupidity of his Watson-like partner, Captain Hastings.

LET LOOSE THE TIGERS
Josephine Cox

Queenie promised to find the long-lost son of the frail, elderly murderess, Hannah Jason. But her enquiries threatened to unlock the cage where crucial secrets had long been held captive.

THE LISTERDALE MYSTERY
Agatha Christie

Twelve short stories ranging from the light-hearted to the macabre, diverse mysteries ingeniously and plausibly contrived and convincingly unravelled.

TO BE LOVED
Lynne Collins

Andrew married the woman he had always loved despite the knowledge that Sarah married him for reasons of her own. So much heartache could have been avoided if only he had known how vital it was to be loved.

ACCUSED NURSE
Jane Converse

Paula found herself accused of a crime which could cost her her job, her nurse's reputation, and even the man she loved, unless the truth came to light.

MORNING IS BREAKING
Lesley Denny

The growing frenzy of war catapults Diane Clements into a clandestine marriage and separation with a German refugee.

LAST BUS TO WOODSTOCK
Colin Dexter

A girl's body is discovered huddled in the courtyard of a Woodstock pub, and Detective Chief Inspector Morse and Sergeant Lewis are hunting a rapist and a murderer.

THE STUBBORN TIDE
Anne Durham

Everyone advised Carol not to grieve so excessively over her cousin's death. She might have followed their advice if the man she loved thought that way about her, but another girl came first in his affections.

SEASONS OF MY LIFE
Hannah Hauxwell and Barry Cockcroft

The story of Hannah Hauxwell's struggle to survive on a desolate farm in the Yorkshire Dales with little money, no electricity and no running water.

TAKING OVER
Shirley Lowe and Angela Ince

A witty insight into what happens when women take over in the boardroom and their husbands take over chores, children and chickenpox.

AFTER MIDNIGHT STORIES,
The Fourth Book Of

A collection of sixteen of the best of today's ghost stories, all different in style and approach but all combining to give the reader that special midnight shiver.

DEAD SPIT
Janet Edmonds

Government vet Linus Rintoul attempts to solve a mystery which plunges him into the esoteric world of pedigree dogs, murder and terrorism, and Crufts Dog Show proves to be far more exciting than he had bargained for . . .

A BARROW IN THE BROADWAY
Pamela Evans

Adopted by the Gordillo family, Rosie Goodson watched their business grow from a street barrow to a chain of supermarkets. But passion, bitterness and her unhappy marriage aliented her from them.

THE GOLD AND THE DROSS
Eleanor Farnes

Lorna found it hard to make ends meet for herself and her mother and then by chance she met two men — one a famous author and one a rich banker. But could she really expect to be happy with either man?

IN PALE BATTALIONS
Robert Goddard

Leonora Galloway has waited all her life to learn the truth about her father, slain on the Somme before she was born, the truth about the death of her mother and the mystery of an unsolved wartime murder.

A DREAM FOR TOMORROW
Grace Goodwin

In her new position as resident nurse at Coombe Magna, Karen Stevens has to bear the emnity of the beautiful Lisa, secretary to the doctor-on-call.

AFTER EMMA
Sheila Hocken

Following the author's previous auto-biographies — EMMA & I, and EMMA & Co., she relates more of the hilarious (and sometimes despairing) antics of her guide dogs.